COMING NEXT TIME...

STORIES! ARTICLES!
SHERLOCK HOLMES & DR. WATSON!

Sherlock Holmes Mystery Magazine #26
is just a few months away...watch for it!

Not a subscriber yet?
Send **$59.95** for 6 issues (postage paid in the U.S.) to:

Wildside Press LLC
Attn: Subscription Dept.
7945 MacArthur Blvd, Suite 215
Cabin John, MD 20818

You can also subscribe online at
www.wildsidepress.com

FROM WATSON'S NOTEBOOKS

Once more Holmes has displayed to me uncharacteristic enthusiasm for this issue of *Sherlock Holmes Mystery Magazine*, which includes three of our adventures, my own "The Adventure of the Priory School," as well as a rendering from my notebook by Paul Hearns, while Bradley Harper has provided an intriguing look at Holmes's nemesis Professor Moriarty.

In addition, my colleague Mr Kaye has included a bit of whimsy by Ed DeJesus and an unusual tale of the American West by Jim Robb. In it events are ably handled by U S Marshal Wyatt Holmes and his friend Dr John Henry Watson. I asked Holmes if he knew of an American branch to his family, but he said no, although it was quite possible. I am inclined to believe it to be accurate, however, because I do know of an American branch of the Watson clan.

The nonfiction section of this issue contains two items concerning my literary agent Arthur Conan Doyle as well as (my blushes) a complimentary discussion of yours truly by one of our regular contributors Gary Lovisi.

And now a few words from Mr Kaye.

—John H Watson, M D

✗   ✗   ✗   ✗

Stories by regular *SHMM* contributors T.J. Glenn, Laird Long and Stan Trybulski will appear in the next issue (#26) as well as a new entry by Steve Shrott. Our occasional editorial assistant Eugene D. Goodwin has another adventure of the Colorado policeman Warren Sutton, while the illustrious Archie Goodwin will provide a new, authorized Nero Wolfe adventure. Finally, two Holmes tales derived from Watson's notebooks have been supplied by our regular writer Jack Grochot and by an East Indian writer S. Subramanian.

Canonically Yours,
Marvin Kaye

✗

SHERLOCK HOLMES
MYSTERY MAGAZINE
VOL. 7, NO. 4   **Issue #25**

FEATURES

NON FICTION

FICTION

ART & CARTOONS

STAFF

Publisher: John Betancourt
Editor: Marvin Kaye
Non-fiction Editor: Carla Coupe
Assistant Editor: Steve Coupe

Sherlock Holmes Mystery Magazine is published by Wildside Press, LLC. Single copies: $10.00 + $3.00 postage. U.S. subscriptions: $59.95 (postage paid) for the next 6 issues in the U.S.A., from: Wildside Press LLC, Subscription Dept. 7945 MacArthur Blvd, Suite 215, Cabin John, MD 20818. International subscriptions: see our web site at www.wildsidepress.com. Available as an ebook through all major ebook etailers, or our web site, www.wildsidepress.com.

ASK MRS HUDSON

by Mrs Martha Hudson

In this issue I include letters that inquire about Mr Holmes's and Dr Watson's preferences in the arts. The recipe I have chosen is a delicious chicken dish stuffed with prunes.

Dear Mrs Hudson,
What music does Sherlock Holmes like best?
Melodically Yours,
Frederick Langelier

✗　✗　✗

Dear Mr Langelier,
I presume your name is a French one, in which case you may be pleased to learn that Mr Holmes is fond of several of that country's composers, including Bizet and Offenbach. This is an exception for him, however, as he is much taken with preclassical compositions by Bach and his sons as well as Vivaldi and Tartini; indeed he often practices playing the Tartini violin sonata commonly called "The Devil's Trill." Mr Holmes says that is aptly named because it is "fiendishly difficult!" When it comes to orchestral music, he is fond of Beethoven and Brahms and is much taken with symphonies of Gustav Mahler and to a lesser extent, those of Anton Bruckner.

Dr Watson tends to romantic music as well as the work of native British composers. He has little patience with some German music and positively detests Wagner.
Melodically Reciprocal,
Martha Hudson

✗　✗　✗　✗

Dear Mrs Hudson,
Are Mr Holmes or Dr Watson much taken by modern art?
James O'Neill

✗　✗　✗

Dear Mr O'Neill,

All art interests Sherlock Holmes, no matter what the period or style. He says Seurat was a genius and finds Marcel Duchamp's bizarre items rather amusing, especially a bird cage holding a cuttlefish bone, what appears to be spilled sugar cubes and a thermometer; it is called "Why Not Sneeze, Rose Sélavey?" (A pun, says Mr Holmes, on "c'est la vie.")

It will not come as a surprise to learn that Dr Watson is much less tolerant of the modernists. He does like French impressionists, though, especially Gaugin, Toulouse-Lautrec and Van Gogh.

Sincerely,
Martha Hudson

✗   ✗   ✗   ✗

Dear Mrs Hudson,

What writers does Mr Holmes like? Also, I ask the same question about Dr Watson ... and what of yourself?

Your Literary Friend,
Sidney Markheim

✗   ✗   ✗

Dear Mr Markheim,

Well may you ask such a question as you bear a literary surname! Its author, of course, is the Scot Robert Louis Stevenson, who Dr Watson and I greatly admire. Both of us have reread *Treasure Island* and that shivery tale about Dr Jekyll and Mr Hyde.

Mr Holmes generally confines himself to nonfiction: all of the newspapers, at least the crime reports, and other work related to his profession. He does like reading philosophy, however, and is especially fond of Joseph Butler, Kierkegaard, Nietzsche and Plato. You may recall that he once recommended as remarkable Winwood Reade's *The Martyrdom of Man*, which he learned about from Dr Watson's agent Conan Doyle.

Sincerely,
Martha Hudson

✗   ✗   ✗   ✗

Does either Mr Holmes or Dr Watson go to the movies? If so, what films have they liked?

(Mrs) Wilmetta Burroughs

✗   ✗   ✗

Dear Mrs Burroughs,

Mr Holmes seldom attends films, not even the one in which he was played by William Gillette. Dr Watson, though, is an avid movie buff and likes nearly everything he sees. I asked him whether he has any favourites and he replied, "I am much taken by stories set in the American West."

Sincerely,
Martha Hudson

✗   ✗   ✗   ✗

The following chicken recipe is easy to do and makes for fine eating. I have served it many times to an enthusiastic Mr Holmes and Dr Watson.

CHICKEN FILLED WITH PRUNES

2 young whole chickens, either broilers or fryers
2 dozen prunes
Orange peel
1 onion, middle-sized
3 tablespoons of butter
¼ cup of sweet red wine
Ginger
Pepper and salt

1. Coat the chicken innards with ginger, pepper and salt.

2. Place 1 dozen prunes inside each chicken.

3. Put 1 tablespoon of butter inside each bird.

4. Cover the chicken breasts and legs with the rest of the butter.

5. Shake pepper and salt over each fowl.

6. Put the birds in a pan with the onion and roast uncovered at 375 degrees for approximately 90 minutes.

7. During the roasting, spoon up the liquid in the pan and pour it over the chickens. Repeat often.

8. When the birds are brown and soft to a fork-prod, take them out and pour the wine over them.

9. Cut chickens in half and place the prunes on top.

10. Cut the orange peel into small pieces. Sprinkle them over the prunes and serve.

SCREEN OF THE CRIME

Sherlock Gnomes (2018)

by Kim Newman

Since anyone reading this is going to be a Holmes movie completist, the question you're all asking isn't "should I go and see *Sherlock Gnomes?*" but "how much pain will I be in while watching *Sherlock Gnomes?*" The good news is: not that much. In fact, you could argue that this kid-friendly comedy take on the Great Detective is closer to the spirit of Doyle than most 21st century big and small screen takes on the Canon—even if it also hinges on that crack in the relationship between the genius and his underappreciated best friend that has become the crux of the drama in so many Holmes movies since *The Private Life of Sherlock Holmes*. It's also an entry in the recent renaissance of British-made family films, which has yielded treasures like the films of Nick Park and the recent Paddington movies... An animated follow-up to *Gnomeo and Juliet, Sherlock Gnomes* isn't quite in that league, but it's the best 'toon Holmes spinoff since Basil the Great Mouse Detective and is studded with easter eggs for Sherlockians (from the Wisteria Lodge flower shop to a cow-shaped bird-feeder called Mrs Udderson). Animation fans will like throwaway products homaging Ray Harryhausen and Karel Zeman (homaged in a soft drink called Zeman and Lime).

It opens with gnomes arguing over which saga is going to get a make-over to follow the treatment meted to Gnomeo and Juliet in the earlier film, and a rapid-fire series of groaner gags proposing *Game of Gnomes, The Twilight Gnome,* etc. before we settle into a world where garden gnomes (kitsch ornaments which are the UK equivalent of pink flamingos) and other decorative figures are alive whenever humans aren't looking at them, and Gnomeo (voiced by James McAvoy) and Juliet (Emily Blunt) are moved to a scrubby London garden with their tribe of supporting players (voiced by the likes of Michael Caine, Maggie Smith, Matt Lucas, Ozzie Osborne, and Stephen Merchant) and get kidnapped. In a prologue, Sherlock (Johnny Depp)—wearing something much closer to the traditional tweed and deerstalker get-up and with a proper beaky profile, albeit with a slight gnomy point to the hat and a chin-beard—and his dumpy, yet dextrous sidekick Watson (Chiwetel Ejiofor, an inspired casting choice)—who seems to have borrowed Daredevil's gadget-packed cane—have a final confrontation with Moriarty (Jamie Demetriou), an evil plastic pie mascot, that seems to be the peak of the detective's career as savior of London's embattled gnomes.

Then, the kidnappings start—carried out, as it happens, by gargoyles named after Ron and Reg Kray (Dexter Fletcher, Javone Prince)—and Sherlock is teased by clues that point to his archnemesis having returned from the grave (if looked at a certain way) and lead him back to the sites of his greatest cases (which are barely sketched in). The A plot—the most rote aspect of the film, and typical of a sequel's need to pick at the scab of the happy ending of the first film—involves Gnomeo sulking because his more competent girlfriend has taken charge of the garden, and Juliet realizing she's being unfair when she sees how Sherlock takes Watson for granted and charges around giving orders and quoting her own dialogue back to her. There's even room for a tiny, serious moment that shows off just how good animated acting can be as Sherlock rattles off a speech about emotion being a handicap in his mission only to show by his subtle expression how he really feels when Juliet clumps off annoyed with him.

At one point, Sherlock's nemesis describes his masterpiece as "the Sistine Chapel of evil plans"—and is annoyed that the heroes have "drawn a cartoon cat on it"—and the film does play fair as a mystery with an intricate storyline that has clues, solutions, several twists and a nice big peril at the end (set around Tower Bridge) that can be averted only by all the heroes doing something spectacular at the same time. The suburban world of *Gnomeo and Juliet* was mostly focused on old-fashioned garden tat—including the various rude novelty gnomes added to the traditional toadstool-sitting fisherfolk in recent years—but this expands to show new types of representative figure—including some priceless business with Chinese cats and a trip to a doll museum where a wasp-waisted, highly articulated Irene Adler (Mary J. Blige) gets to sing about her frustrations with Sherlock. Yes, it's a musical too—the film was produced by Elton John and David Furnish, and is soundtracked with cleverly-adapted snippets of the Elton John/Bernie Taupin back catalogue that somehow fit in perfectly with the spirit of the thing. Directed by John Stevenson, who has worked on the Muppet franchise and in various capacities on things like *Count Duckula* and *Felix the Cat*, but hasn't directed a feature since *Kung Fu Panda* (2008).

Sherlockians of a collection-minded bent will, of course, notice that there's a lot of sweet *Sherlock Gnomes* merchandise about—including, naturally, Sherlock and Watson plush gnomes, a puzzle-book and a novelization.

⚔

Kim Newman is a prolific, award-winning English writer and editor, who also acts, is a film critic, and a London broadcaster. Of his many novels and stories, one of the most famous is *Anno Dracula*.

"THE ADVENTURE OF THE DANCING MEN" MANUSCRIPT SOLD AT AUCTION

by Stan Trybulski

A signed, handwritten manuscript of Sir Arthur Conan Doyle's Sherlock Holmes story "The Adventure of the Dancing Men" was sold April 18 at Heritage Auctions in Dallas, Texas for $312,500 to an anonymous collector.

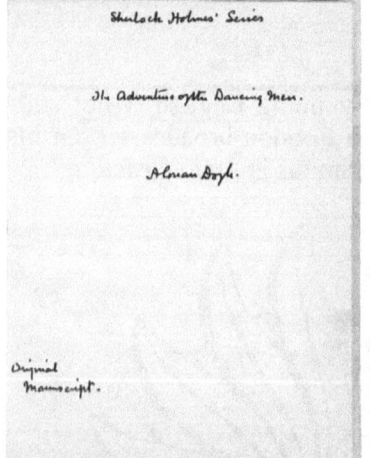

The 53-page manuscript was written by Conan Doyle in the late spring of 1903 at Undershaw, his country home in Waverly, Surrey. Only one of two Sherlock Holmes stories in which the great detective's clients die (the other is "The Five Orange Pips"), it was published simultaneously in the December, 1903 issue of *The Strand Magazine* in London and the Dec. 5, 1903 issue of *Collier's Weekly* in New York. In 1905, it was included as the fourth story in the 13-story anthology *The Return of Sherlock Holmes*.

Conan Doyle had long pondered writing a story centered on ciphers. In May 1903 while staying at The Hill House Hotel in Norfolk, he signed a young woman's autograph book. The autograph book also contained drawings made by two children, Gilbert John Cubitt and Edith Alice Cubitt: decorated letters by Gilbert to make a secret writing and stick figure musical notes by Edith on a five-line musical stave. Conan Doyle combined these ideas in the story and in an effort to honor Gilbert and Alice, he named his client Cubitt.

"The Dancing Men" manuscript was written on the recto of wide-ruled paper and includes stick figures sketched by the author. It also contains many hand-written emendations by Conan Doyle and three autographed signatures: on the cover page, on the title page and in a holographic epilogue.

The handwritten manuscript left Conan Doyle's possession in 1918 when he donated it to an auction to raise funds for the British Red Cross. It was purchased and resold several times before winding up in 1974 in the possession of Brian Perkins, a Texas book dealer. Heirs of Perkins placed the manuscript up for this week's auction.

The images of the title page and page with dancing figures are courtesy of Heritage Auctions.   ✗

Stan Trybulski, who wrote *One Trick Pony* and other crime novels, was a Brooklyn felony trial prosecutor before he went into private practice. He says that he now divides his time between France and "two acres of Connecticut tranquility".

TRUE BELIEVERS: LOOKING AT CONAN DOYLE'S GHOST STORIES

by Leah Guinn

Everyone knows that Arthur Conan Doyle "killed" Sherlock Holmes. And everybody knows why. Tired of being associated with his detective and yearning to write more "important," literary fiction, he arranged to have our hero tumble to his death over a waterfall, leaving him free to devote himself to historical epics.

This is true, of course, in a very simplistic fashion. However, what people often seem to forget is that the Sherlock Holmes stories were not the only short, slightly pulpy tales that Conan Doyle wrote. A quick look at his bibliography reveals a long list of offerings with titles like, "The Great Kleinplatz Experiment," "The Brazilian Cat," and "The Horror of the Heights," all of them of a sensationalistic nature, and making their appearances in magazines from the very beginning of his career, in 1879, to the very end, in 1930.

The stories vary in content. Many are crime stories, some involve horrible creatures, some are examples of early science fiction, and in quite a few of them, one can find echoes of cases solved by the inhabitants of 221B. Not surprisingly for a man who both enjoyed scary yarns and joined England's Society for Psychical Research, a significant handful of them are also ghost stories. Entertaining and frightening without being gruesome, they have, for the most part, held up well over the years. But taken as a whole, they reveal more than just whose reflection appears in the silver mirror, or why the first brown hand wasn't good enough. It seems possible, using his tales of phantoms, to catch subtle glimpses of Conan Doyle's evolution from fascinated skeptic to dedicated spiritualist. Every writer leaves traces of himself in his work; it's inevitable. In Conan Doyle's stories, we can get an idea of his personal experiences, as well as catch a shift in his view of ghosts themselves.

Conan Doyle submitted one of his first attempts at short fiction, "The Haunted Grange of Goresthorpe," to *Blackwood's* in 1879, where it promptly disappeared, only to be discovered in the archives decades later. A brief, eerie story, it features two old school friends who decide to spend the night in a haunted house. Jack, on whose property the old manor house stands, is a physician who prides himself on his practicality and views the neighbors who tell stories about the Grange as having "untutored minds." When Tom Hulton comes to visit, Jack is slightly disturbed by the "strange speculative way of thinking" his friend seems to have picked up during his time in Germany, and which is particularly evident when the topics of ghosts and spiritualism come up.

Hulton tells Jack that there are two kinds of people: "the men who profess not to believe in ghosts and are mortally afraid of them, and the men who admit at least the possibility of their existence and would go out of their way to see one." Tom, who is definitely the latter, is eager to spend the night at the Grange, while Jack, the non-believer, has definite misgivings.

And so Conan Doyle sets up the situation: a skeptic and a believer, with at least one hoping to prove himself right. Biographer Andrew Lycett points out how neatly these characters reflect Conan Doyle's own struggle at the time. Not content with his family's Catholicism, yet unwilling to be a materialist, he was at his own spiritual crossroads, although he would arrive at his conclusions after years of thought and exploration, rather than with the horrible visions of one night.[1]

Of all the stories appearing in this essay, "The Haunted Grange of Gorsethorpe" is probably the most frightening. It is a traditional haunted house story, with a tragic, albeit ancient backstory, in which a previous tenant hacked his two children to death and strangled his wife. There is the requisite atmosphere of an abandoned house, the infectious excitement and anxiety of the ghost hunters, strange sounds and a creeping sense of menace before the horrible vision. After that, the story ends abruptly, with Jack and Tom, as per haunted house convention, never speaking of what they've seen. In this story, ghosts are scary, they have been cursed

---

1   Lycett, Andrew. *The Man Who Created Sherlock Holmes: The Life and Times of Sir Arthur Conan Doyle*. New York: Free Press, 2008, p. 66.

to relive their final terrible moments, and there is no real interaction with the observers. Tom and Jack are scared and disturbed, but don't seem to achieve any greater enlightenment, other than the realization that ghosts exist. Despite the set up, it is a story meant purely for entertainment.

1883's "Selecting a Ghost" has a different tone entirely. Where "Goresthorpe" is dark and atmospheric, this story is funny, as the reader comes to realize that "Argentine D'Odd," as Silas Dodd prefers to be called, has pretensions to a feudal Norman heritage that is almost certainly not his. D'Odd has got his manor but, unfortunately, not the ghost he believes should come with it[2]. He just assumed one would be included, and now he is consumed with jealousy as his neighbor, Farmer Jorrocks, complains about his own ghost, a theatrical young woman whom D'Odd believes the man does not deserve. Eventually, he takes his wife's advice and calls on her cousin. If the man discovered their coat of arms and series of family portraits, surely he can procure a ghost.

So it is that "Argentine" finds himself sitting in the middle of his soon-to-be-haunted dining hall in the company of one Mr. Abraham, a 'ghost dealer.' After drinking a potion to ensure he will be able to see into the spirit realm, he watches as specter after specter enters the room and describes his or her qualifications. Just as he makes his choice, however, he hears his wife cry out that they've been robbed. D'Odd then consults a medical doctor, who informs him that the potion contained chloral, and the ghostly visions were a product of his own dreams.

The phantoms in this story, therefore, are imaginary, and the "medium" a fraud and criminal. Everything has a logical explanation and D'Odd, by his own admission a true believer, is made out to be a fool. This story was written during the time Conan Doyle was working as a doctor in Southsea and experimenting with table rapping alongside other curious friends. While he obviously enjoyed his little psychic investigations and doubtless hoped to see or hear something unusual, he is not emotionally invested in their outcome and again, requires nothing of this story than it be entertaining enough for publication.

---

2   As the original Goresthorpe manuscript had vanished, as far as Conan Doyle knew, he happily re-uses the name for this house.

In 1899's "The Brown Hand," a physician's well-meaning actions lead to his being haunted for years. The story's narrator, Dr. Hardacre, an amateur psychic investigator, relates how his uncle, retired and ailing physician Sir Dominick Holden, asks him to sleep in his home laboratory so that he might see for himself the vision which has tormented him nightly since his days in India. Hardacre does, indeed, see the ghost—an Indian man in a gray gown who enters the lab, surveys the jars of pathology specimens, then throws up his hand (for he has only one) and vanishes. We learn the next morning that the performance begins by his shaking Sir Dominick's shoulder, and that he is, as one might expect, searching for his missing hand, removed in a long-ago operation. The nameless Indian wished to keep the diseased hand, so that he could be buried with it, as his religion required the body to be intact. Ever helpful, Sir Dominick offered to preserve the hand and keep it safe in his lab; unfortunately, however, its jar was one of many lost in a massive fire. Look as he might, the ghost will never be able to find it. Hardacre comes up with a creative solution: why not bring in a similar hand from a morgue as a substitute? This works … eventually … with the end result being that Hardacre becomes his uncle's most trusted advisor and inherits his considerable estate after his death.[3]

In the story, Dr. Hardacre states that he is a member of the Psychical Research Society—an obvious alteration of the SPR (Society for Psychical Research) of which Conan Doyle himself was a member. He also mentions that he had investigated a haunted house with two other members, and experienced nothing "exciting or convincing." This again echoes Conan Doyle's own experience: in June of 1894, he joined Frank Podmore and Dr. Sidney Scott on a similar venture. According to the official report, the "poltergeist" was actually a member of the household; in later years, however, Conan Doyle claimed otherwise during his spiritualist lectures, whether through actual belief or wishful thinking is anyone's guess.

---

3   Although the story first appeared in the *Strand Magazine* in 1899, it was also published in *Tales of Twilight and the Unseen*, which was published in 1929. The story may have been revised somewhat at the time, accounting for Hardacre's mention that his aunt and uncle died in the great flu epidemic.

This is, at any rate, Hardacre's first ghost, and it is an interactive one. Unlike the haunts of Goresthorpe Grange, who behave almost like paranormal recordings, this spirit has consciousness of itself, its mission, and others. It also can take solid form—at least enough to shake Sir Dominick and to grab hold of its new hand. It displays emotions other than anguish and terror; it can feel hope, frustration, anger, and happiness. It is, then, a very *human* spirit, and while Sir Dominick, likely tormented by his own guilt and helplessness, is worn down by its visits, Dr. Hardacre and the reader end up with a certain amount of affection for it—possibly as the author intended.

Not that all is rosy in human-spirit interactions. In 1900's "Playing with Fire," Conan Doyle addresses the potential dangers of the séance. In his spiritualist writings, he often discussed the ways in which skeptics could sabotage a session with a medium, thereby forcing him or her to resort to fraud in order to maintain some credibility. In this story, however, he takes the opposite tack: exploring what could happen when séances go wrong.

Or only slightly wrong, anyway. Conan Doyle's characters in this story seem to be set up as common spiritualist "types." There is the dogmatic believer, the open-minded friend, the dilettante always ready to hear "some new thing," and the amateur medium. On this night, however, they have a guest—a true student of the occult who tells them that he wishes to take them a bit further, with an experiment. "Thoughts are things," he admonishes them, and as such, can be materialized. A realistic séance sequence follows and, without revealing too much of the denouement, this is precisely what happens. Interestingly, however, Conan Doyle decides to pull his punch, and while the incident would likely be scary enough should it happen in real life, most readers could probably dream up better ways to make "Playing With Fire" truly frightening. This, of course, begs the question: did Conan Doyle the nascent spiritualist decide that making a séance actually dangerous would betray the faith he would soon claim as his own? Did he worry about painting the men and women he was coming to know personally as foolish or even wicked? "Fortunetelling" was illegal in England, after all, and he may have been concerned that in turning this story into a horror tale, he would bring more negative attention on mediums— particularly if readers began to wonder if "Playing With Fire" was based on a true story. This is, of course, conjecture, but it does not seem an unreasonable one.

Conan Doyle had a particular interest in psychometry—the ability to receive impressions from objects about the people who owned or touched them. He uses this phenomenon in at least three stories: "The Leather Funnel" (1902); "The Silver Mirror" (1908); and "Through the Veil" (1910). In each story, the main character is transported back in time to see, in varying degrees of detail, an event in history. For the narrator of the first, most disturbing, story, this is the torture of the Marchioness de Brinvilliers, forced to drink two gallons of water poured down her throat through the funnel in question. The overworked, sleep-deprived protagonist of the second story sees the murder of David Rizzio, the Italian-born personal secretary (and rumored lover) of Mary, Queen of Scots, reflected through the mirror that had once witnessed the actual event. "Through the Veil" goes even further. In this story, a man and woman touring an old Roman fort at Newstead on their first anniversary are transported back—first through the fort and its artifacts, and then through dreams—to the moment when, in their past lives, he, a native Scot, took her for his own, accidentally killing her Roman husband as the fort was overrun and burned.[4]

Although the incidents depicted are violent, the stories themselves suggest that psychic abilities can be used as a tool—a way to look into the past. This is in line with Conan Doyle's own belief that, rather than arresting mediums, the police should employ them to solve crimes.[5] When mystery author Agatha Christie disappeared for eleven days in December of 1926, Conan Doyle got a glove from her husband which he gave to psychometrist Horace Leaf. Leaf, who didn't know the glove's source, made several observations and predictions Conan Doyle enthusiastically claimed to be accurate. Again, through these later stories, we see his growing acceptance and portrayal of paranormal abilities as positive, even romantic, phenomena.

In the end, however, what are ghosts, really, but the spirits or (for the more materialist believer) impressions of people who have died? Most ghost stories, being written by the living, focus on that

---

4   At least for the purposes of the story. The fort existed, but the attack and fire seem to be purely fictional.

5   Imagine Sherlock Holmes hearing that!

particular demographic and its experiences when exposed to the afterlife's creepier aspects. The final tale in this discussion takes a slightly different tack.

"How It Happened" was first published in early 1918. Like many of Conan Doyle's stories, it draws on some personal experience—this time, his car accident in March, 1904 when, with his brother Innes in the passenger seat, he managed to run into the gate outside Undershaw and flip the vehicle. Both men were pinned under the car, and Conan Doyle believed the only thing that saved him was the steering wheel, although it later snapped. Fortunately he and his brother emerged with only a few painful bruises and went golfing again the following day.

Such is not the case with our narrator. Arriving at the train station after a day's trip into London, he finds his new car waiting for him—a 30 horsepower Robur. He has a chauffeur, and he's never driven this car before, so it does cross his mind that he should perhaps wait until morning to get acquainted with it, but like any boy with a brand new plaything, he wants to try it out.

All goes well until his gearshift sticks as he starts to head down a steep hill. His brakes begin to fail and he loses control of the car. He hopes that, through steering, he'll be able to take the car around three curves and through the gate of his home, but it's all very dicey, and at one point, both he and his chauffeur, Perkins, take turns trying to persuade each other to jump out. They hit the stone pillar in an open car at 50 mph.

The narrator is thrown from the vehicle. When he comes to, his first concern is Perkins. The chauffeur seems to be all right; he is conscious and talking, asking after "master," and while the car overturned, it has only pinned his leg. The rescuers' attention is focused on him, and upon something in front of the car; they pay the narrator no mind, but "master" is not alone. His friend Stanley is there with him. It is only after a few minutes that he realizes how impossible this is.

> "Stanley, you are dead."
> He looked at me with that same old, gentle wistful smile.
> "So are you," he said.

By 1918, Conan Doyle was a committed spiritualist. Two years before, he writes in the final chapter of his autobiography, "I began a campaign … which can only finish when all is finished." He would boldly declare the truth of spiritualism in the face of those who believed it to be anti-religious, anti-scientific, or simple charlatanism.[6] So it is that, although "How It Happened" is a moving tale, it is also, we are informed at the beginning, delivered through a medium during an automatic writing session. Just as his old friend Stanley appeared to usher the speaker into the afterlife, he in turn is reassuring the reader that he also has nothing to fear. Summaries of the story typically mention that it is about the dangers of male bravado, or a tale of loyalty, but it is neither. It is Conan Doyle telling us that there is life after death.

"How It Happened" has a poignant *coda*. Both Conan Doyle's eldest son, Kingsley, and his brother, Innes, died of influenza within months of each other: Kingsley in October of 1918, and Innes the next February. In March, 1919, Conan Doyle had a session with one of his trusted mediums, Annie Brittain, who put him in touch with his son. According to biographer Andrew Lycett, Kingsley told his father that Innes, upon first seeing him, said "'I thought you were dead,' to which Kingsley had replied, 'Just as dead as you are.'"[7] Had Mrs. Brittain read her client's story? One has to wonder.

The horror writer H.P. Lovecraft famously wrote, "The oldest and strongest emotion of mankind is fear, and the oldest and strongest kind of fear is fear of the unknown."[8] For human beings, death and what comes after are, even with religious guidance, ultimately unknowable. This is why horror stories don't deal with grocery shopping, or romantic picnics or conversations about football, because none of those are intrinsically frightening. Introduce a ghost into one of those scenarios, however, and it immediately becomes scary. Why? Because a ghost is *dead*. It is the unknown reaching

---

6   *Memories and Adventures*, p. 396. It is probably worthwhile to note here that "Stanley" died in the hospital at Bloemfontein, of enteric fever. Was he based on one of Conan Doyle's actual patients? We can't know.

7   Lycett, p. 401.

8   Lovecraft, H.P. "Supernatural Horror in Literature," available online here: hplovecraft.com/writings/texts/essays/shil.aspx

into our lives and, if we are particularly unlucky, it might want to take us back with it.

In Arthur Conan Doyle's ghost stories, there seems to be a clear progression between the scary, unknowable ghosts who haunted Goresthorpe Grange, and Stanley, the familiar, albeit dead, friend. Mediums evolve from thieves who dope up their victims to the automatic writer who helps "master" deliver a coherent account of his own passage into another life. Even when a séance goes wrong, it simply makes a mess, rather than unleashing a troop of demons on the world. It would be naïve to claim that Conan Doyle did not have a slight agenda as he wrote these stories—particularly the last. Of course he did. As a self-appointed spokesman for spiritualism, he wanted people to share and be comforted by his beliefs. But even if he weren't of such an evangelical bent, it is likely that his ghost stories would have taken a similar turn. They no longer focus on fear because their creator is no longer afraid. They show a comprehensible afterlife because he was certain of one. He firmly believed that through the means provided by spiritualism, the dead he knew, loved, and trusted had told him so. As another of his creations once said, "There is nothing like first-hand evidence."

✗

Leah Guinn is the co-author, with Jaime Mahoney, of *A Curious Collection of Dates* (Wessex Press). She reviews pastiche for "The Well-Read Sherlockian." A member of the Illustrious Clients of Indianapolis, she lives in Indiana with her husband and three children.

WATSON—THE PERFECT PARTNER!

by Gary Lovisi

Did you ever wonder… Suppose Author Conan Doyle had not chosen Dr. Watson as the partner for Sherlock Holmes? Doyle could have chosen someone else to partner with his Great Detective. It did not have to be Watson. So, if not Watson, then who else might fit the needs of Holmes as the perfect partner?

As Doyle was creating the character of Sherlock Holmes and was choosing a partner for his Great Detective, he knew he needed to pick someone who could showcase Holmes's unique talents to the world, but also a person who brought value to the relationship—someone who would be an important and intrinsic part of the Holmes team. And Holmes and Watson are a team, make no mistake about that! However, it was not all that easy for Holmes to find the right person to share rooms with, and get along with—or perhaps more importantly, someone who could get along with *him*!

"'I'VE FOUND IT! I'VE FOUND IT!' HE SHOUTED."

Holmes could be a difficult person to be around. He could be moody, arrogant, and troublesome. He kept odd hours. He test fired weapons indoors. He was also brilliant, but in a rather annoying way that most regular people would not accept or ever put up with for very long. Holmes was unique. Thus any person Holmes would share rooms with, must be unique as well.

Sherlock Holmes also did not have *friends*, at least not in the way we commonly think of friends. His *friends* were more likely associates, a network of people used in his work to close cases; some members of the official police; criminals (reformed, such as Shinwell "Porky" Johnson, and others not reformed); the Baker Street Irregulars, even Toby the dog was a part of his "team" at times.

With all that known, when Holmes was looking to share the rooms at 221B Baker Street with another person, he knew it must be someone who would be able to tolerate him and his odd manners—no easy feat—and more so, to be of value to him in his important work. The list would seem to be rather short, but there are some likely candidates.

Putting Watson aside for the moment, Holmes (through Doyle) could have chosen someone from another profession to be his partner. With that possibility in mind, is there someone other than Watson, or a medical doctor, who might have brought more to the table for Holmes?

There are other candidates, of course, other than good old Watson. Men of other important professions had much to offer. Perhaps a Scotland Yard Inspector? Or some young and talented constable? Perhaps a knowledgeable lawyer? A local politician? Or even a newspaper reporter? Men from each of these professions, or others, would bring experiences and contacts that would prove an important contribution to Holmes and his work.

Let's take a look at an official detective. Lestrade certainly would not be the man here, but another one of them might fit in well and have much to contribute to Holmes. A Scotland Yard Inspector could certainly grease the skids for Holmes with The Yard, and offer Holmes unique inside access to crime scenes, records, suspects and all that! Perhaps? Or perhaps not, since early on in his career the official police did not understand nor respect Holmes and his methods, nor appreciate what he was doing in his new consulting detective service. The feeling was mutual. Holmes looked upon the official police, including vaulted Scotland Yard Inspectors as plodding, unimaginative, incompetent and generally useless in solving crimes. The official police more often than not ignored or mucked-up key evidence at a crime scene—and sometimes even arrested the wrong man! No, there was no way that Holmes could ever share rooms with a member of the official police. He did not respect them—and they did not respect him—certainly not in the early days of his career.

Now a lawyer, or even a local politician might offer some good advice with the law or help in cutting red tape, and both would certainly have valued connections. However, Holmes did not need the advice of any lawyer to tell him why he could *not* take a certain action in his work. Nor did he need to listen to any self-serving politician. He did not trust or respect such men. Besides, he had Mycroft to turn to for any serious legal needs or when he needed to access political juice.

However, as for Holmes sharing rooms with his brother, Mycroft, or teaming up with him—forget about that! They were brothers and sometimes associates, but they could never live together, nor be partners. They could barely tolerate each other!

Now a newspaper reporter might be an interesting choice. A competent writer and investigative journalist just might offer some positive contributions as a partner to Holmes, and a crime reporter even more so. The thought is intriguing. Even a muck-rake journalist of the so-called popular press might offer value by being able to reach into certain dark places, or contacting the right people to solve a crime. In fact, Doyle used exactly this device in the story of another of his famous heroes—newshound Malone in *The Lost World* played a definite Watson-like role as he told the story of Professor Challenger, and his unique talents and adventures. However, Holmes did not need to room and partner with a newspaperman, as he had access to them quite readily when needed. He also had access to many of the same contacts any good newshound would have. So a newspaperman's qualities might actually be redundant. Also newspapermen could be very aggressive and such a man might reveal too much information, too soon, on his cases. Holmes could not abide that, so a journalist would not do.

So who then? For Holmes there is much to consider in choosing someone to share his work and life. This can be complicated because no one more than Holmes knows the dangers that a partner can be put in because of his line of work. Holmes deals with criminals and murderers all the time. These are enemies who would take revenge against him, and it is a fact he lives with every day. It is one reason, I believe, why Holmes does not involve himself romantically with the opposite sex. It is not because of some ill-gotten misogyny against women at all, in fact he loves and respects women—though he also knows they can be dangerous. Even deadly. However, Holmes knows that by becoming romantically involved with any woman, he would worry about her safety all the time. Holmes is aware any woman he loved would always be in danger and his enemies would seek to target her, to get to him. Any child born from such a union would make the danger far worse! Such a situation was unconscionable. Holmes could never allow anyone he loved to be placed in such mortal danger. Certainly not a woman he loved. So he closed that part of his life. Holmes gave up a lot in the pursuit of his profession. However, he still needed to find someone to share the rooms at 221B with, and that person would have to be someone special. Perhaps exceptional.

So what is it that makes Watson the perfect partner for Sherlock Holmes? We can trace the clues early on. They appear in the very first Sherlock Holmes story, *A Study in Scarlet*. Here, even before Stamford introduces Watson to Holmes, he tells Watson he knows a man who is looking to share rooms. Watson replies:

> "By Jove!" I cried, "if he really wants someone to share the rooms and the expense, I am the very man for him. I should prefer having a partner to being alone."

Already—even before he meets Holmes—Watson is thinking of Holmes as a potential *partner*! It is interesting that he uses that very word. However, in the very next paragraph of the story, Watson is warned.

> Young Stamford looked rather strangely at me over his wine-glass. "You don't know Sherlock Holmes yet," he said, "perhaps you would not care for him as a constant companion."

Once Watson is introduced to Holmes they speak about the rooms and the issue of compatibility comes up.

Sherlock Holmes seemed delighted at the idea of sharing his rooms with me.

"I have my eye on a suite in Baker Street," he said, "which would suit us down to the ground. You don't mind the smell of strong tobacco, I hope?"

"I always smoke 'ships" myself," I answered.

"That's good enough. I generally have chemicals about, and occasionally do experiments. Would that annoy you?"

"By no means."

"Let me see—what are my other shortcomings? I get in the dumps at times, and don't open my mouth for days on end. You must not think I am sulky when I do that. Just leave me alone, and I'll soon be right. What have you to confess now? It's just as well for two fellows to know the worst of one another before they begin to live together."

I laughed at this cross-examination. "I keep a bull pup." I said, *[Never again mentioned by Watson, G.L.]* "and I object to rows because my nerves are shaken, and I get up at all sorts of ungodly hours, and I am extremely lazy. I have another set of vices when I am well, but those are the principal ones at present."

Holmes was looking for a man who would be able to put up with his unique eccentricities, but who can also contribute to his work. That is where Watson comes in. John Watson is a retired army medical doctor whose military medical knowledge adds significantly to Holmes's own. In fact, Watson brings vast medical knowledge to the table—and while Holmes has a middling amount of knowledge in this area—Watson is an expert in the field and his opinion is invaluable to Holmes in the examination of bodies and determining time and mode of death.

Furthermore, Watson as a military man, has seen active service in the front lines in Afghanistan, a particularly brutal war. He has been wounded. He has treated the wounded on the battlefield. He has seen all types of serious injuries and bullet wounds. His medical knowledge is vast and deep and of inestimable value to Holmes— and Holmes knows it! Watson has seen war and action up close. He is brave and loyal. He still has his army service revolver—which

Holmes is aware of and often asks him to carry along on dangerous cases. In other words, Holmes knows that Watson—who he can count on as a *de facto* enforcer—is brave and loyal and will not shirk at the sight of action or violence. Watson is steadfast. Watson can also take care of himself with a gun, he is not afraid to use it when necessary, and he is brave under fire. These are valuable assets to Holmes. He respects Watson's abilities.

However with Watson, Holmes gets much more. Watson is a good man, honest, trustworthy, he has a sense of humor, a well-rounded personality, and he is easy to be around. He is also a very decent fellow. The two men just naturally become good friends and get along well. These are character traits Holmes especially values, and they grow their relationship and friendship into a true partnership. And while Holmes took precautions when it came to Watson's safety, he had confidence in the doctor's ability to handle himself in any situation.

Furthermore, Watson is a writer, and he writes up Holmes's cases and has them published in the popular press to world-wide acclaim. He does this to showcase his friend's great talent and unique abilities. While Holmes allows these published reports of his cases so as to popularize his methods as a consulting detective—he is also serious about these reports so that law enforcement can improve by learning his methods. Holmes even writes and publishes his own monographs upon certain aspects of detective work. His well-known study of cigarette ash is a detailed and highly instructive work allowing the reader to determine exactly what type of cigarette a criminal may have smoked just from the remains of the ash. Using this information, cigarette ash at a crime scene can offer an important clue in finding a killer. Furthermore, Holmes himself wrote at least one of his own cases for publication in *The Strand* magazine under Watson's name, ("The Adventure of The Lion's Mane", from 1907, but published in 1926). So we know that Holmes was not averse to having his methods, or knowledge of his cases made public, and Watson's write-ups of his cases fulfilled this desire admirably.

I believe that no matter how much Holmes protested Watson's use of melodrama in the writing of some of his cases, The Great Detective secretly enjoyed the acclaim and attention Watson's chronicles brought him in the popular press. The writing and publication in *The Strand* of these cases by Watson warms Holmes's ego, it is a recognition of his life and work, and I believe it means more to Holmes than he would like to admit.

After Watson moves in with Holmes he comments on his new roommate in *A Study in Scarlet*.

> Holmes was certainly not a difficult man to live with. He was quiet in his ways, and his habits were regular. It was rare for him to be up after ten at night, and he had invariably

breakfasted and gone out before I rose in the morning... Nothing could exceed his energy when the working fit was upon him, but now and again a reaction would seize him, and for days he would lie upon the sofa in the sitting-room, hardly uttering a word or moving a muscle from morning to night.

Obviously the two men are compatible. In the above statement Watson is being more than generous in his thoughts on life with Holmes. Their partnership and friendship grow over the years as Watson continually surprises Holmes with his loyalty, bravery, medical knowledge, and his writings of important cases—all of which show his devotion and admiration of Holmes. In fact, Holmes and Watson get along smashingly!

For Sherlock Holmes—there surely is no other choice—Watson is the perfect partner!

Gary Lovisi is an MWA Edgar-nominated author for his Sherlock Holmes pastiche "The Adventure of The Missing Detective." He is a Holmes fan, collector, and writes various articles and short stories of, and about, The Great Detective, some of which have appeared in this magazine. He is the editor of *Paperback Parade* and *Hardboiled* magazines, and of the Sherlock Holmes anthology, *The Great Detective: His Further Adventures* (Wildside Press). You can find out more about him and his work at his website: www.gryphonbooks.com, or on Facebook.

CONFLICTED FEELINGS: ARTHUR CONAN DOYLE & SHERLOCK HOLMES

by Janice Law

One of the sad facts of the literary business is that authors tire of characters. No matter how successful or delightful one's heroes, sooner or later their adventures seem repetitious and their quirks, irritating. The Muse departs and their continuation becomes wearying.

But Sherlock Holmes's case presents some interesting features. As early as 1891 Conan Doyle was writing to his mother—then and until her death, his chief confidante—that he had in mind to slay Holmes. Fans of the Great Detective can be thankful she reacted with horror.

The stories continued for the moment, but two years later on a hiking trip in Switzerland, he discussed Holmes's death with his companions and the Reichenbach Falls were suggested as a venue. By December, he added two words to his diary: "Killed Holmes." Outcry ensued.

In the immediate aftermath, Conan Doyle declared that he'd had an "overdose" of Holmes and compared the experience to eating too much *fois gras*. Twenty-six stories were enough. Three years later at the Author's Club, he claimed extravagantly that Holmes's death was not murder but justifiable self-defense: "… if I had not killed him, he would have killed me."

Conan Doyle was able to ignore the public dismay and the pleas of his editors but not financial realities. His family was large and largely poor. His wife's health was declining, he had young children and a great personal need for activity and adventure. Money was required. Holmes returned for the most famous of his cases, *The Hound of the Baskervilles*, and later for other adventures, all to the author's great profit.

Still, he remained ungrateful.

When William Gillette requested alterations in Conan Doyle's stage version, he telegraphed the American actor: "You may marry him, murder him or do anything you like with him."

Clearly the Holmes stories were not as close to Conan Doyle's heart as his "serious work," the historical novels and the later volumes on spiritualism. Indeed, he felt that Holmes kept him from "higher things" in the literary realm and perhaps in another realm as well, for the Great Detective's relentless logic and materialism only partially reflected his author's mind.

An excellent mind it was, too, capable of seeing weaknesses in a much-touted tuberculosis cure (by the great Robert Koch, no less), clearing several people falsely convicted of crimes and producing a trenchant analysis of British military medicine during the Boer War. He foresaw the dangers of submarine warfare and campaigned for better equipment and protections for British soldiers and sailors. In these matters, he was all Holmes.

But another side of his character, equally powerful and deeply rooted, was a hunger for spiritual experience. Raised a Catholic, he wrote an ecstatic letter to his mother about receiving his first communion. This childhood piety was literally beaten out of him at a harsh Jesuit boarding school. Modern science, led by Darwin, finished orthodox Christianity forever without destroying a longing for something transcendental.

His solution was an exploration of the thickets of Victorian alternate spirituality, first very much in the spirit of scientific inquiry via séances, experiments with table rapping, ghost hunting and membership in the Society for Psychical Research. Significantly, he later resigned from this body, citing their "skepticism."

Holmes, naturally, is exceedingly skeptical where paranormal phenomena is concerned. He doesn't believe in ghosts or vampires or a Hound from Hell and when he comes up against the Baskerville's phantom dog he soon lays bare the-all-too human agents behind what are some of the creepiest phenomena in literature.

It's a wonderful performance, but maybe an ambiguous joy to his author, who was increasingly absorbed in spiritualism. Faced with the long terminal illness of his first wife, his father's confinement and death for alcoholic dementia, the premature death of his oldest sister, and the huge World War I losses, including his oldest son and his brother, Conan Doyle increasingly sought solace in the afterlife and in continued communication with the dead.

He saw spiritualism as a new stage in religion and the comforts of spirit communication as a public good. Despite loss of friends and the damage to his intellectual and literary reputation, he devoted the energies of his last decades and much of his fortune to the promotion of his beliefs.

It is sad to read his defense of the evidence of fairy folk presented in *The Coming of the Fairies,* which he took as further evidence of a transcendental spiritual world. The scientist remains in his careful recording of camera settings and apertures, but science and logic are quite lost in the spiritualist's refusal to see that the goblins and fairies look suspiciously like cut-out paper figures.

Holmes would not have made such a mistake. It was perhaps not just the difficulties of constructing the detective's adventures or a fear that the great man might outstay his welcome that motivated Conan Doyle's repeated efforts to rid himself of his most popular character. Holmes represented, in exaggerated form, the author's own critical intellect, the intellect that helped him to fame, influence and wealth, but which threatened the spiritual cravings of his personality, cravings that with age and loss grew ever more pressing.

Ironically, the exaggeration of the analytical mind that made Sherlock Holmes so distinct and so memorable was to become an uneasy intellectual conscience for a man abandoning science, materialism and logic. Conan Doyle was, in a sense, destined to be haunted by his own outstanding creation.

✗

Janice Law writes novels and non-fiction as well as short stories. Her most recent books are *Homeward Dove* (Wildside) and *Mornings in London* (Mysterious Press), the last installment of her Lambda award winning series featuring the gay, alcoholic painter, Francis Bacon.

WHY SHERLOCK HOLMES WON'T DIE

by Jacqueline Seewald

Sherlock Holmes, more than any other fictional detective, has achieved immortality via books, short stories, radio, TV, the theatre, and motion pictures. I recently read *A Study in Scarlet Women* written by Sherry Thomas, published by Berkley, the first in the Lady Sherlock Series, which offers yet another fresh mystery-twist version on this fiction phenomenon.

Not only has mystery and detective fiction been influenced by the legendary Holmes, but also other fiction genres as well. Genevieve Cogman, who writes a well-reviewed fantasy series, started reading Sherlock Holmes stories at an early age. In her debut novel, *The Invisible Library*, which received a starred review from *Library Journal*, Cogman introduces a private detective named Vale, who is described as similar to Sherlock Holmes. Cogman sets her fantasy in an alternate world which is similar to late-Victorian London. Mr. Vale is enlisted to help the librarians locate a rare book, and along the way solve some murders.

Sherlock Holmes has been played by a host of well-respected actors, which includes Basil Rathbone (my personal favorite), Orson Welles, Charlton Heston, Christopher Lee, Roger Moore, Leonard Nimoy, and John Cleese. Robert Downey, Jr.'s film versions were highly successful, while Benedict Cumberbatch played Holmes in the BBC series *Sherlock*, which aired in America on PBS. Jonny Lee Miller stars as a modern-day Sherlock Holmes—Brooklyn, New York based—in the popular CBS series *Elementary*.

If Sherlock Holmes has captured the popular imagination ever since the Victorian era, the credit belongs to his creator, Sir Arthur Conan Doyle, upon whom the spotlight rightfully shines. *Arthur & George*, a Public Broadcasting series encompassing a three-part Masterpiece mystery, aired in 2015, based on a novel by Julian Barnes. Martin Clunes of *Doc Martin* fame starred as Doyle. The novel was based on real facts in Doyle's life and was a finalist for the Man Booker Prize.

How Sherlock Changed the World, another Public Broadcasting program, featured dramatized excerpts from several of Doyle's stories. Sherlock Holmes used chemistry, bloodstains, and fingerprints to catch offenders. In many ways, the modern detective can be seen as a direct extension of Conan Doyle's literary genius. Using interviews and archival materials, this program did an excellent job of exploring real crimes that were solved thanks to techniques, equipment, or methods of reasoning Holmes used.

Conan Doyle did an extraordinary job of demonstrating how forensic evidence could be used to solve crimes. He was critical of the police of his time and Holmes, his detective, reflects this viewpoint. Apparently, Conan Doyle often received letters appealing for help with crimes. Because of one letter, Doyle decided to act as a detective himself. In 1903 his shrewd observations and experience as an eye doctor helped exonerate a man accused of brutally killing animals in a Staffordshire village. However, although Doyle proved the accused man innocent, the police refused to believe it. The experience caused Doyle to become influential in setting up the first official British Court of Appeal two years later.

Sherlock Holmes's extraordinary powers of observation were created by the mind of Conan Doyle and still influences people to this day. NBA Hall of Famer Kareem Abdul-Jabbar wrote an article entitled "Why We Love Sherlock Holmes" for the September 27, 2015, issue of *Parade Magazine*. He described being fascinated by Holmes's insistence on logic and facts as the wisest means to form opinions. It influenced his approach to basketball as he practiced powers of observation on his opponents, scoping out their moves, habits, strengths, and weaknesses in careful detail. He began studying clues, expanding his intellectual horizons. He even co-authored a novel entitled *Mycroft Holmes*, based on Sherlock's brother.

Sir Arthur Conan Doyle actually tired of writing the Holmes stories, which he felt kept him from concentrating on more serious historical writing. "The Adventure of the Final Problem" was published in December of 1893 in *The Strand* magazine. In this short story, Doyle killed off Sherlock Holmes. He had Holmes tumble to his death from the Reichenbach Falls in the northern Swiss Alps, which Doyle visited that year. Holmes was locked in a death struggle with the villainous Professor Moriarty. The reaction of readers? *The Strand Magazine* lost 20,000 subscribers. According to legend, fans of Holmes took to the streets wearing black armbands.

In 1901, Conan Doyle brought Holmes back in *The Hound of the Baskervilles*. However, he made it clear that this story preceded the death of his famed detective. *The Hound of the Baskervilles* was also originally published in *The Strand*. Public reaction was overwhelming: The magazine's circulation rose by thirty thousand overnight. Thus it would be no surprise that Conan Doyle would bring Holmes back to life at least in part to please his enthusiastic fans. He did so in "The Adventure of the Empty House." Watson finds out Holmes's death was just a ruse to hide from Moriarty's associates.

Altogether, Conan Doyle wrote fifty-six Sherlock Holmes short stories and four novels: *A Study in Scarlet* (1887), *The Sign of the Four* (1890), *The Hound of the Baskervilles* (serialized in 1901-1902), and *The Valley of Fear* (serialized in 1914-15). These are considered classics. The influence of Conan Doyle's Sherlock Holmes stories continues in today's media. Just tune in to any of the forensic police dramas on television and you will see it. The legacy lives on.

Multiple award-winning author, Jacqueline Seewald, has taught creative, expository and technical writing at Rutgers University as well as high school English. She also worked as both an academic librarian and an educational media specialist. Seventeen of her books of fiction have been published to critical praise including books for adults, teens and children. Seewald's mystery novels include the Kim Reynolds series. Her most recent mystery novel is *Death Promise* from Encircle Publishing. Her short stories, poems, essays, reviews and articles have appeared in hundreds of diverse publications and numerous anthologies such as: *The Writer, L.A. Times, Reader's Digest, Pedestal, Sherlock Holmes Mystery Magazine, Over My Dead Body!, Gumshoe Review, The Mystery Megapack, Library Journal, The Christian Science Monitor* and *Publisher's Weekly*. Her blog can be found at: http://jacquelineseewald.blogspot.com

EDINBURGH TWILIGHT, BY CAROLE LAWRENCE

A BOOK REVIEW

by Eugene D. Goodwin

Though I usually avoid thrillers about serial killers, *Edinburgh Twilight* is an exception for two reasons. It is a well-written and fascinating story, first of a proposed series, set in Edinburgh in 1881, and its author is a *Sherlock Holmes Mystery Magazine* regular contributor, having written both stories and essays for our pages. The byline is Carole Lawrence, which is a family name of Carole Buggé. In *SHMM* she has written several excellent Sherlock Holmes adventures and wrote two Holmes novels for St. Martin's Press: *The Star of India* and *The Haunting of Torre Abbey*. She also did three "cozy" mysteries for Berkley, the provocatively-titled *Who Killed Blanche DuBois?*, *Who Killed Dorian Gray?* and *Who Killed Mona Lisa?* Her fantasies have appeared in *Weird Tales*.

The protagonist of *Edinburgh Twilight* is twenty-seven-year-old Detective Inspector Ian Hamilton, a man haunted by the mysterious fire that killed his parents. One day a young man's body is found just below Arthur's Seat, the old mountain dominating Edinburgh's eastern extremity. At first the death is considered a suicide, but in spite of his superior's impatience with Hamilton, the inspector is sure the victim was strangled. It soon becomes clear that he is correct as the body count escalates and the citizens become terrified and demand action from the police.

A curious aspect of the murders is that a strange grisly playing card is found on each body. As he investigates, Hamilton is aided by an aunt with a gift for photography and a librarian fascinated by the criminal mind. Things become more complicated when Ian's estranged brother shows up to complicate his life. Tension mounts as the "Holyrood Strangler" adds more victims to his toll and in the process deliberately draws closer to his nemesis Ian Hamilton.

I found *Edinburgh Twilight* compelling and difficult to put down—"just one more chapter" turning into nightly marathons. A great deal of its suspense is the growing fear that one of the characters one has come to admire may be the next victim and this does indeed happen.

The novel is available in paperback and Kindle editions. Its author informed me that she has already written the next Ian Hamilton thriller.

⚔

Gene Goodwin is a fan of Colorado, since that's where he learned to love TexMex food.

THE OLD POLICEMAN

by Paul Hearns

1913

I have rarely been tasked with setting down an account of my own inquiries as my colleague and friend Dr Watson has usually obliged in this respect. It is even rarer that I am tasked with setting down the facts in so unusual a case as one which presented itself in my retirement.

Working one morning in May, I had a full pipe which was serving admirably to subdue my bees as I experimented with the relative merits of a Warré hive over a traditional skep as used by the ancients. As the bees were almost at the height of their activity, I was immersed in my observations and almost took no notice of the figure that approached up the path.

When finally I did turn my attention towards him, I observed him to be a man in his late sixties, though still hearty, with near full facial hair and a ruddiness to his complexion that betrayed certain habits. He had the unmistakable carriage of a policeman.

As I had to return certain elements of the Warré to their proper configuration, I had only the briefest opportunity to discern that this man had been a detective at least and found lucrative employment beyond the force on his retirement.

"Good day to you, sir. Mr Holmes, I presume?"

His accent still had traces of his birthplace about it, and I placed him not entirely remote from where we stood: a Dorset man, though not rural, who spent much time in London and some in high society.

"It is, Inspector, and whom do I have the honour of addressing?"

He noted, though was not surprised by my address, and proceeded with grace.

"My name is Frederick Abberline, formerly Chief Inspector at Scotland Yard—"

"And of H Division," I took up, "having been distinguished in the Cleveland Street affair before taking up for the Pinkerton Agency in London and abroad."

He faltered for a moment, as my slow recall dragged my mind away from my apiarian observations, but again proceeded with grace.

"Mr Holmes, you have me at once."

"Inspector," I began again, as the title seemed to please him somewhat, "I am aware of a great many officers of the police from my time as a consulting detective—a time which is long since at an end."

"Well, perhaps, Mr Holmes, if I might entreat you, there is one more case to which you might turn your mind. I can pay you well for your trouble, as I have enjoyed good professional engagement since my time with the force."

"Inspector Abberline, I do not believe we crossed paths during our respective careers, but my practice, when I did such work, was never to alter my fees, save when I omitted with them altogether."

"Nonetheless, sir, I was a professional and I would extend the same respect due another."

"Indeed, Inspector. But I am now retired, as are you. My bees are very busy currently, and my observations are at a most critical juncture."

"Begging your pardon, Mr Holmes. I do not wish to intrude, were it not for necessity driving me. I humbly ask, as one who has spent his life in service of the law, to another who has given of himself for that same end, for your help in one final matter."

I turned my attention from the hives again toward the figure that stood between me and sun, which was almost at its zenith. There was an earnest look about the Inspector's face which was at once compelling to me and unfamiliar to him.

"Perhaps, Inspector, I could offer you some refreshment. The day is warm, and luncheon is almost upon us, though I must warn you, I live alone, and my housekeeper is an infrequent visitor."

Inside the house, with tea upon a tray and a few morsels of bread, cheese, and cold meat, we regarded each other in the relative gloom of my sitting room, where the May sunshine found little ingress.

The Inspector was clearly ill at ease, though had an air of determination that meant he was intent upon his course.

"Thank you, Mr Holmes, for hearing me out. I am most grateful."

"I have agreed to nothing yet, Inspector, beyond ensuring you do not go hungry from my house."

"Still, sir, I am grateful."

He drew a deep breath and exhaled in the manner of one about to begin a confession.

"You know something of my career, Mr Holmes, but while I was with the Met, before Cleveland Street, there was another case with which I was associated. One which did not have so satisfactory an outcome.

"I was at Scotland Yard when the Whitechapel Murders began in August of 1888. I spent ten years in H Division, as you rightly recall. I was ordered back there in September to take charge and bring the murderer to justice.

"There were many good men working in H Division at the time, many of whom I trained myself or saw coming through the ranks. I was confident that with good police work and vigilance and some small bit of luck, we would catch the madman and if not hang him, then at least ensure his butchery was brought to an end.

"But that was not to be. The case proved to be a strange one and while there were suspects and arrests, I believe we never laid hands on the actual killer."

There the Inspector paused and looked again at me with that expression.

"Ah yes," I said, "the Whitechapel Murders—a grisly affair. I remember being fascinated in a professional sense, but being otherwise occupied at the time and frequently beyond these shores, I did not tax myself with it, believing that such instances are best solved by the likes of Scotland Yard and the hard work of the regular police force."

"Well, Mr Holmes, I too believed at the time that hard work, thorough investigation and good correlation would yield the right man, but as you well know, that was not how it came to be."

The Inspector paused and looked at me.

"But what do you want of me, Inspector?" I asked. "We are hardly about to catch a train to London and hope that the streets of Whitechapel will yield clues nearly twenty-five years on."

"No, Mr Holmes, that is not my proposal. What I ask is altogether different. I have enjoyed a good career as a policeman and beyond. I received commendations and awards on many occasions, more than most I'll wager, but the case that haunts me still is that of the terrible name of Jack the Ripper.

"Many of my colleagues since, both above and below me, have named names and listed suspects who have been taken up by newspaper men and hacks that have created what can only be called fanciful solutions to this old case.

"Each time I hear mention, I return to my notes and recollections and I wrack my brain to see if there might be some grain of truth to them, a possibility that there might be some hope of at least putting a face to that awful name.

"Some years ago at my home in Bournemouth, a newspaper man for the *Pall Mall Gazette* put to me a whole host of names that some now call suspects, some of whom I never heard tell of. I remained steadfast in my opinion that we were no nearer then than in those dark days of '88 to naming the killer, but as I began to consider those possibilities, I found myself questioning much of what I'd done before."

The Inspector stopped speaking. He looked down at his china tea cup and remained motionless for some time.

Eventually, he laid aside the tea and picked up the fine coat, unusually heavy for the time of year, that he laid over the back of his chair. From an inside pocket he took a large leather wallet that was tied with a thong, bursting with assorted leaves of paper and not a few photographs.

The Inspector sat forward in his chair and held the wallet in his hands as though he were about to make an offering. He looked at me directly.

"I have here my notes of the case, Mr Holmes, with many of the documents concerned. Some of them are originals, some are copies—all are accurate. I would hope that together with these and my recollections, I could lay the case before you.

"I would hope that you can tell me, sir, not the name of the man, but whether I—"

"Whether you *could* have caught him?" I asked.

"Yes. As one professional to another, I ask you now to help me know if we missed something, if I missed something—if I let the maniac go free."

I looked down at the empty grate of the fire and wished for another pipe.

"Inspector," I said carefully, "this type of crime, it is not my area of expertise. It is, as I thought at the time, best suited to the regular police and their wide resources in local engagement and detection. At this distance—"

"But Mr Holmes, we *failed*. I knew those streets and I knew those people. For ten years I caught the worst that Whitechapel had to offer and put them before a judge. I believed that we never came close to this man, and I know … I *think* that we did all we could."

"And yet, Inspector, you find yourself moved to ask a stranger to review your work—to point out your flaws."

"Indeed, sir, to have such observations from someone of your standing would be an honour. In my work since the force, I have come to have a greater understanding and respect for the consulting detective. I only wish that we could have had your service at the time. Your name was mentioned many times at the Yard at the time, but never having directly observed your work, I am sorry to say, I dismissed such talk."

I allowed myself a smile.

"Inspector, you are not to be criticized for such a decision. I believe in your position, given your responsibilities, I might well have done the same."

The light in the room was changing already and though it would be bright for many hours yet, I already felt the creep of night.

The Inspector lowered his gaze again and stared now at his worn leather wallet.

I longed to return to my bees and yet I sensed there was something else, some other thing driving this honest man in his endeavour. There seemed an urgency to his request not borne of the unguarded recollections of colleagues or the solicitations of newspaper men.

I picked up my pipe and tapped it out, letting the silence remain otherwise unbroken as I prepared a charge.

When it was lit and a good head of smoke produced, I spoke again.

"I hope that your collection and recollection are comprehensive, Inspector. As a detective, you will know only too well how dangerous it is to reason from insufficient data."

The Inspector looked up and smiled at last.

"Comprehensive indeed. Encyclopaedic, if I may say."

"Very well, then."

"And where shall we start, Mr Holmes?"

"Where one must always start, Inspector: with the evidence!"

"The best evidence in this case is undoubtedly the victims, Mr Holmes. Let us start there."

"Agreed."

"The body of Martha Tabram was found in a stairwell in George Yard Buildings at 4:45 a.m. by one Alfred Crowe, a resident, on his return from work. From the evidence of another resident, the body may well have been there since 3:30 a.m. The woman had thirty-nine stab wounds, all but one of which appear to have been inflicted with the same knife.

"The knife was likely a common penknife, though a singular wound to the sternum appears to have been made with a larger weapon, possibly a dagger or bayonet. The victim's throat showed signs of manual strangulation."

I listened as the Inspector gave detailed accounts of the victims, and I clouded the room with a heavy pall of tobacco smoke. He listed six in all.

As the Inspector spoke, he sat back in his chair, looking more comfortable than he had since I first set eyes on him.

He relayed the details and leafed through the wallet, sometimes taking up a page or photograph and laying it on the table or the floor before him. He rarely seemed to have to consult the pages as the details appear to have long been committed to memory.

When finally the Inspector paused, he leaned back in the chair and rested for a moment.

I could not complain at the level of detail with which I was furnished, and apart from the odd clarification here or there on some point or detail, let the Inspector go on as he would.

Now I stood rubbing my temples, a cold pipe still in my teeth, ready to begin the process of deduction.

"You named six victims, Inspector, though there are doubts over two, at least, if we are to assume the work of a single hand."

"Indeed, Mr Holmes, both Tabram and Stride pose problems if we're to look at the cases all together—hind-sight is a wonderful perspective."

"That it is, Inspector, but logic and reason are even better."

"Let us take the key points here: the killer of Nichols, Chapman, Eddowes, and Kelly cut the throat right around and down to the bone, with evidence of attempts to separate vertebrae. All but Kelly showed signs of strangulation before the throat was cut, though this may also have been the case with her, too. Where indications were apparent, the throat was cut from left to right."

"That is correct, sir."

"But Tabram, though, showing no sign of cuts to the throat, was strangled also."

"Correct, and while she had abdominal wounds, they were primarily of a stabbing nature, as opposed to the evisceration and mutilations of Eddowes, Chapman, and Kelly."

"And Stride did not show manual strangulation evidence but could have been throttled with her own scarf. She did show signs of physical force upon her shoulders, and a reduced, but still fatal, cut to the throat from left to right."

"That is correct, Mr Holmes."

"All of these women were known to have practiced as prostitutes, all were murdered at night without a sound and in public, but secluded areas.

"Inspector, I ask you to draw upon your experience in H Division. Have you ever known two murderers to be at work on the same class of victims simultaneously in such a small area?"

"I have never encountered such thing, but then again, Mr Holmes, before that time I had never encountered a man who went about murdering strangers."

"Ah, we must be careful, Inspector, not to infer what we cannot prove. Your own account suggests that while these unfortunates frequented the same streets and possibly the same public houses, there is no evidence from which to conclude that they knew each other or not. Therefore, with a similar lack of evidence for the killer, it is impossible to say whether he knew them or not. For my part I have not seen many killers who murder strangers, but it has been a rising phenomenon in our crowded cities in recent times with many such cases emerging. I would hazard that our Jack is an early instance of this terrible development. In those cases of which I have read, it seems to be a downward path that the maniac follows, but one that often starts with lesser crimes. Though it is impossible to say with certainty, I would contend, on balance of probabilities, that Tabram was the first killing by this man's hand, but that he also killed Stride and was disturbed in the act. The killer may well have hidden in the yard with Stride, blending into the crowd of onlookers that assembled. This Jack has control of his nerve, as all of his crimes are high risk and yet nowhere in the evidence does there appear an account of a panicked individual fleeing or the hurried disposal of evidence."

"True, Mr Holmes. The impression is one of a maniac of most singular nature who seems to be able to steel himself for these terrible crimes and then rein himself in to make his escape through the streets."

"Let us make the reasonable supposition that the killer's first murder was Tabram, that he killed Stride and was disturbed before he proceeded to Eddowes and ultimately Kelly."

"Indeed, Mr Holmes, I would agree. There were later killings, but none have the true ring of the Ripper about them. Though the murder of Alice McKenzie in '89 and Francis Coles in '91 have similarities, they are distant and detached."

"Proceed then with the witnesses, Inspector."

With the same level of detail, the Inspector recounted the major witnesses and referred to the excellent work of then Chief Inspector Swanson as he summarized the information for his superiors. The inspector focused on two key witnesses who had each observed individuals with two of the victims hours before their grim encounters. One of which led, unfortunately, to a dark turn for certain sections of the community.

"So, despite the apparent confederate observed by Israel Schwartz in the company of Elizabeth Stride, it is your opinion, Inspector, that the address of 'Lipski' was directed at Schwartz himself and not at this perceived accomplice?"

"That is my view, sir. I worked those streets since the Lipski murder trial and heard it used as a derogatory term on many occasions. I fear the second man may well have been an innocent, too, driven away for fear of being embroiled in an altercation, as Schwartz himself did. For though he thought he was being pursued, Schwartz spoke little English and when he looked back was alone."

"Excellent, Inspector. Then let's proceed."

The Inspector went on to describe testimony of Joseph Lawende, who saw a man conversing with a woman who fitted the description of Catherine Eddowes, mere minutes before the body of that unfortunate was found in Mitre Square.

"He said that the man was about five feet seven inches in height, about thirty years of age and of fair complexion with a fair moustache. He looked shabby and had a salt and pepper coloured coat and flat peaked cap with a red kerchief about his neck.

"Schwartz said that the pair were—"

"Lawende, Inspector," I interjected.

"Yes, Lawende," he continued, "said that the pair were talking quietly and that he would not be sure he could recognize the man again. Though when he was pressed, Schwartz said—"

"Lawende, surely?"

"Yes, of course. Lawende," said the Inspector, "gave further details but, again said that he wasn't sure he would know the fellow again."

"Inspector, we have been upon this for some time now," I observed, as the sun had now quite deserted the room. "Perhaps some more refreshment might help in our work."

The Inspector looked at me with a most puzzled expression.

"I assure you, Mr Holmes, I am quite ready to continue, that is, if you are ready to do the same."

I regarded the man's indignant look before turning back to the cold grate, leaning an elbow on the mantle.

"Proceed then, Inspector, with all haste."

We examined for some time more the witnesses from police reports, the coroner's court, and even those attempts that were made to identify suspects long after the fact. The Inspector detailed the most secret attempt to have a witness identify an inmate of Colney Hatch asylum, but time and memory were not favourable to the efforts.

"Inspector, your recall is excellent, but I fear that there is little to be had from these accounts. From the evidence of the victims and what we know of these types of crimes, we can safely say that the man will be of the same, or slightly elevated, class as his victims. He is at least twenty-five, though probably more than thirty, he has a job that is, at best, semi-skilled, and lives and works in the area from which the victims are drawn. He is of the same race and does not look in the slightest out of place in the environs where he chooses his victims. If I recall the streets of that locale well enough, he would frequent the lodging houses of the likes of Flower and Dean Street, or Dorset Street. He is unlikely to have a wife, though that is not impossible. More likely is that he lives with some family, a mother, perhaps, or siblings. He will be a somewhat anti-social character but will have, probably through his work, the ability to pass himself in his society. He appears to be able to have the women accompany him willingly and when his ghoulish work is complete, he makes his escape through the same streets where he hunted, largely unobserved. From all of this we can deduce that he is at home in these streets, has a deep knowledge of the locale, its workings and its dangers. He takes extreme risks in the time he has available and yet when time is short, or circumstances threaten, he can rein himself in to avoid detection and give later vent to his urges. I disagree with the opinion of the medical examiners of a building pattern of mutilations, for if you look at each crime, as best we can, where time allowed, the mutilations were extensive. Where time was not a factor at all, as in the case of Kelly, Jack gave fullest vent to his fury and yet the mutilations still have a consistency about them that mark them out as by the same hand.

"This man, this Jack the Ripper," I said, "dehumanizes his victims by attacking their sexuality as well as their identity and key traits. He mutilates, eyes, ears, cheeks, and even lips, though hands and fingers appear only ever to have defensive wounds. I would reason that this man never experienced sexual intimacy, as the focus of his attention on the organs of sexuality betray a mind that never understood them in their sexual context, but rather only in their anatomical sense."

"He had on several occasions taken away organs—wombs and kidneys," said the Inspector in a hollow tone. "But how are we ever to recognize these things in a suspect?"

"Well, Inspector, let us look at the best of your suspects now and see with whom we can reconcile, if any, these ghastly traits."

"A later colleague, Mr Holmes, who was not even part of the force at the time, has suggested a young doctor who was suspected of solitary vices. This chap called Druitt was favoured because he was fished out of the Thames not long after the killing of Mary Kelly."

The Inspector detailed this case and several others: one Thomas Cutbush; a tall American called Tumblety; a feeble-minded man called Kosminski; Hutchinson, who was a consort of the victim Mary Kelly; and a convicted poisoner, Severin Klosowski, also known as George Chapman.

"In all you have detailed, Inspector, I agree. We can rule out the young doctor, Cutbush, and the tall American—what little we can say of the killer does not tally with any of these. Kosminski simply does not fit the kind of dementia that the killer displays, as one thing is certain—it is his rigorous self-control that allows him to commit his crimes and that was not at all true of Kosminski."

"All of which brings us to Chapman," he said gravely.

The Inspector now betrayed a certain partiality, which caused me no little concern.

"Chapman was a piece of work, Mr Holmes, a nasty piece of work. The way that he could look on as he caused his wives to waste away in agony was cold, Mr. Holmes. I believe such a man is capable of anything."

"Indeed, Inspector, I do not doubt that Chapman was capable, but these killings bear a signature, as did Chapman's own. I doubt that they are the same author. Look at the facts, Inspector. Chapman arrived in London barely a year before the first murder. His known places of work are not at the heart of the streets that the killer so obviously knew and of which he made such skillful use. Though the witness statements sometimes give us a dark mien, many say fair, and none remark on a noticeably foreign accent. And as for the use of poison as a weapon, Inspector, well, that is an area of expertise of mine. One of the most remarkable women I have ever known was hanged for poisoning three children. It is an intimate weapon, one that is often used where the killer knows the victim and can watch as the effects become obvious and take their course. But a knife, Inspector, in these cases, I believe, is an extension of the killer and so its use can be seen as an altogether different type of intimacy. No, Inspector, though it is not unheard of for a killer to change his methods as he learns and develops, the particular mania of this man only takes full expression in cutting and ripping. It is the act which gives him satisfaction, not the victim or the hunt—hence his pursuit of another victim after being interrupted with Stride. Chapman killed to rid himself of an inconvenience when he got bored of his wives and they became obstacles. Jack killed to provide the canvas on which he wrought his terrible signature."

"But, Mr Holmes, Chapman had the anatomical skill, he was present in the London locale at the time, he was a known and multiple killer, and his attack upon his wife in America with a knife before he ever used poison—"

"Inspector, everything you say is fact!" I interjected. "But I must impose the rule of logic. Chapman is unlikely to have had sufficient local knowledge in '88, he is unlikely to have sufficient English, either. He would hardly have established so distinct a signature only to revert to the wild passions of domestic abuse a year after murdering Mary Kelly. And finally, he is unlikely to have so vented his fury and satisfied his lust that he was able to forego his knife for the poison bottle seven years later. All these unlikelihoods, Inspector, combine to tell me that Chapman was at the time a nascent killer and one of altogether different mettle. He has not the stripes of your Jack the Ripper."

The Inspector drew back, somewhat less than crestfallen, but disabused, I hoped, of what was clearly a long-held notion. "I'm sorry, sir. But I must argue to the contrary. Chapman is a stronger suspect than your Kosminski, who appears a mere harmless idiot!"

"I assure you, Inspector, I do not hold with Kosminski as a suspect at all."

"As well you shouldn't, for he is nothing of the sort!"

The Inspector leaned forward in his chair, the ruddiness in his cheeks giving way to a rising scarlet.

"All this time you've argued for Kosminski over Chapman, ignoring the evidence I've placed before you. You write your reports and tell Sir Charles that we do sterling work and yet you discount the very fruits of those labours!"

The Inspector was in full flow now and his eyes looked at me with a fury that seemed misplaced. I listened as he berated someone else for their directing of the case; by the sound of it, with some justification.

As with a somnambulist discovered in the act, I realized that the Inspector was not here in this room on the Sussex Downs, but back in a London office, probably before his Chief Inspector, arguing the case for his long-held favourite, against the odds, it seemed.

After fully expressing his frustration and throwing several more aspects of his theory into the bargain, he eventually relaxed, satisfied. "Respectfully, sir, I believe you are wrong and the facts of the case, when we collar this Jack, will bear me out!"

The Inspector took his handkerchief from his pocket and wiped his brow. He folded it carefully in a manner that marked a practiced gesture, probably his method to calm himself when he lost his temper, and then looked at me as I stood facing him. His eyes immediately registered a change. He looked me up and down and then grasped the arms of his chair tightly as he cast about the room and took in his surroundings. He drew several quick breaths and tensed, reeling from the realization.

When he looked at me again, the colour had drained from his face, leaving a ghastly pallor. He swallowed hard and tried to steady himself. His manner betrayed that this was not the first such turn he experienced.

"I am sorry, Mr Holmes. I have quite lost the thread of what I was saying. You had said of Chapman that—"

"Please, Inspector, let us dispense with Chapman and Whitechapel for a moment."

The Inspector shrank visibly.

"How long have you suffered these … turns?"

He paused for a moment, but made no attempt to evade the question.

"A little over a year now, but they were infrequent at first."

"I am not a medical man, Inspector, but I believe the recent work of Dr Alois Alzheimer has done most to describe your condition."

"Indeed, it was that doctor's name that my own physician cited."

"A terrible condition, Inspector."

At last it was clear what brought this man to me. While a professional doubt developed with friends and colleagues playing detective long after the fact, clouding reality with their idle musings, this terrible affliction meant that peace of mind may well have eluded him, too.

"I can recall the very last detail of my cases, Mr Holmes. I can see the faces of suspects, I can hear the voices of my men report, and recall the smell of the charge rooms, but when I take a turn I cannot find the kitchen in my own house. I have become lost sometimes, when I recall a case, repeating conversations that I've had on the matter."

"I believe that you were just now tackling Chief Inspector Swanson and his favouring of the suspect Kosminski."

The Inspector shrank again.

"I have relived that one many times, I fear."

"I am so very sorry, Inspector. I understand your horror at this most awful prospect."

The silence that followed was almost unbearable. We contemplated what we both knew to be inevitable. I must admit, in an entirely selfish way, I was glad to have seen this manifestation that I might know the signs, for I knew the condition leads inexorably in a slow descent to dementia. I bit harder on my cold pipe than was altogether necessary, and for the first time in many years wished for my favoured solution to relieve this horror unleashed in my mind.

Eventually I was compelled to speak and do some small thing to alleviate the weight of the situation upon the Inspector.

"Sir, it is my most considered opinion, given the facts that you have placed before me, that you did not directly encounter the murderer known as Jack the Ripper in your investigations. Furthermore, I do not believe that the methods at your disposal at the time would have yielded the man, given what we can establish of him. Nothing you have presented from your work or the musings of your colleagues since would convince me they have come any closer than you did to the killer's identity. I cannot say whether I would have caught the man, for your methods are not mine. But this I can say: I believe that you did, at the time, all you could with the resources and the methods at your disposal. I am afraid, Inspector, no more than that can be said with certainty."

The silence descended again and we each contemplated our work. Inwardly, now that I was more fully acquainted with the case, I was gladdened to have been so engaged at the time as to be kept away from Whitechapel. What was all the more surprising was that I had not heard from my brother Mycroft on the matter, as the rumblings back and forth between Commissioner Warren and his superiors, as far as the prime minister, must have been most unsettling.

After a long period of private contemplation, I again felt compelled to break the silence.

"You are welcome, Inspector, to rest for whatever is left of the night, though I see already a grey line on the horizon. There is a room on the left at the top of the stairs that I believe you would find adequate."

"You are most kind, Mr Holmes, but if I might simply rest here a moment, I shall be on my way," said the Inspector wearily. "I am most grateful for your help in this matter, Mr Holmes, and I feel a great deal unburdened. My … condition has made me doubt much of my faculties in this matter lately and I am best pleased to have been able to lay out a clear account for you, whatever your conclusions."

"You are welcome, Inspector. I am only sorry that I could not have provided more comfort in those conclusions."

"They were as much as I could have hoped for."

And with that I bid the Inspector good-night.

I went to the scullery where I kept tobacco for refilling my slipper. I lit another charge and put on my mantle to take a turn upon the Downs.

The morning air cleared my head and the pipe calmed my mind, perturbed as it was by the prospect of such an affliction laying low a keen professional mind.

On my return, I found the chair in my sitting room empty, with only the stale smell of smoke and empty cups left to bear witness to the night's revelations.

✗

Paul Hearns is a journalist and writer, living and working in Dublin, Ireland. Married, with three children, he writes speculative fiction in the benevolent shadow of Le Fanu, James, Lovecraft, and of course, Doyle.

THE ADVENTURE OF THE BORDER CONVENTION

by Jim Robb

With a sure-footedness born of long practice, the conductor walked down the aisle of the swaying railway car as it sped across the Kansas plains on a sunny spring day in 1884.

"Excuse me, sirs," he said to the two men in the dark three-piece suits. "Would one of you be Wyatt Holmes, U.S. Marshal?"

"I am," the larger of the two said. He was tall and dark-haired with the muscular build of a boxer. His less-than-handsome face was much improved by a large handlebar moustache. On his head was a black Stetson with a flat brim and a flat crown. He wore a pair of unusual-looking revolvers slung low on his hips.

"I have a telegram for you, Marshal," the conductor said. "The telegraph agent gave it to me in Dodge City."

"Thanks," Holmes said. He handed the conductor a coin and waited for him to continue down the aisle before opening the envelope and reading the message.

"Change of plans, Doc," he said to his colleague.

Dr. John Henry Watson was almost as tall as Holmes, but here the resemblance ended. He was slender and unhealthy-looking and wore a more modest moustache. His unruly ash-blond hair was only partially tamed by a black derby hat. A Schofield revolver rode on his right hip. "We aren't going to Washington after all?" he asked, his accent revealing his Georgia origins.

"According to this, we're needed in Brownsville. You used to live in Texas. How hard is it to get there from here?"

Watson thought for a moment. "Well, if we get off this train in Emporia we can take the Missouri Kansas & Texas Railway as far as Denison, just south of the Red River. The Houston & Texas Central Railway will get us from there to Galveston, on the Gulf of Mexico. Then we'll have to travel by ship down the coast to

Port Isabel, but we can take the Rio Grande Railroad from there to Brownsville."

"So not hard at all," Holmes said. "I wonder why we're needed in Brownsville, of all places?"

✗   ✗   ✗   ✗

Bell clanging, the train from Port Isabel pulled into the Brownsville station. Behind the diamond-stacked locomotive were two tenders, the first piled high with mesquite wood, the other carrying additional water for the thirsty iron horse. A few assorted freight cars trailed behind and a short passenger coach brought up the rear.

Holmes and Watson climbed down from the coach as soon as the train clanked and hissed to a stop. After arranging for their luggage to be delivered to their hotel they set out on foot, following a tramway line that ran down the middle of Twelfth Street. They walked perhaps half a dozen blocks before Holmes pointed out a saloon that would have looked more at home in New Orleans than in Texas.

"What do you think, Doc?" Holmes said.

"It has been a very long trip," Watson said. "I don't think anyone would blame us if we enjoyed a drink or two."

They walked up to the bar and each ordered a whiskey. With drinks in hand, they turned and surveyed the room.

"So, Holmes," Watson asked, playing their usual game, "what do you observe about the people here?"

"You see those two fellows cheating at poker over there? They held up a stagecoach a while back. Also, the man at the end of the bar to your right escaped from prison not long ago and he's been rustling cattle ever since."

"You never cease to amaze me, Holmes. How were you able to deduce all of that?"

"Elementary, Doc," Holmes replied. "I saw their pictures on wanted posters when we changed trains in Houston."

Holmes set his drink on the bar and walked up to the men at the card table. "Tom Ketchum and Bud Upshaw, my name is Wyatt Holmes. I'm taking you in for armed robbery."

The two sprang up and reached for their pistols, but before their weapons were clear of their holsters, Holmes's revolvers were trained on them. The two badmen froze.

"I wouldn't be doing that if I was you," Holmes said.

"You ain't even cocked them guns of yours," Ketchum said.

Holmes pointed a pistol at the floor between Ketchum's feet and pulled the trigger. With a loud report the weapon fired. Ketchum jumped back three feet and snatched his hand away from his own weapon.

"All right, all right," Upshaw said, raising his hands as well. "You got us." At a gesture from Holmes two bystanders came up behind them and relieved them of their weapons.

"Ruben Burrow," Holmes said without turning around, "you're under arrest, too, for being unlawfully at large and for cattle rustling."

Another gunshot rang out, but Holmes showed no sign of being startled. "Keep them covered, boys," he said and turned to see Burrow slumped on the floor with his head and left shoulder resting against the bar.

"He must have thought he got the drop on you," Watson said, returning his Schofield to its holster. "I can't imagine why."

"Is he going to be all right?"

"I should think so; I shot him in the arm. I do believe he has fainted."

A man wearing a sheriff's badge stormed into the saloon, followed by two deputies. "What is going on here?" he asked. His hoarse, high-pitched, Spanish-accented voice sounded like a saw hitting a spike.

"Everything's under control, Sheriff," Holmes said. "There's three men here that belong in jail cells, but that one will need a doctor first."

The sheriff organized a party to carry Burrow to the doctor's office and another to escort Ketchum and Upshaw to the jail, with a deputy in charge of each. Then he turned his attention towards Holmes. "I am Santiago Brito. Unless I am greatly mistaken, you are Wyatt Holmes, yes?"

"Guilty as charged. This is my deputy, Dr. John Watson."

"I am pleased to meet you, Dr. Watson," Brito said.

"Call me Doc," Watson said.

"I publish *El Demócrata*, the local Spanish-language newspaper," Brito said to Holmes, "and your picture has appeared many times in its pages. That engraving was the best investment I have ever made. Many people have purchased my newspapers just for your picture, because the *Daily Cosmopolitan* and my other English-language competitors cannot print one. My typesetter always keeps it within reach against news of your latest exploits in Arizona. And speaking of that, what brings the two of you here, so far away from Arizona?"

"We're not sure," Holmes said. "We're supposed to meet Agent Ross of the United States Secret Service at the Miller Hotel. Where is that, by the way?"

"It is on Elizabeth Street, a few blocks that way," Brito said, pointing, "a large three-story building that looks like a Spanish mission—you will know it when you see it. It is by far the finest hotel in town. You can have your boots polished overnight and left outside your door and have the newspaper of your choice delivered to your room every morning. But my curiosity gets the better of me. May I ask what kind of pistols you are carrying?"

"They're prototype Webley revolvers with seven-and-a-half-inch target barrels," Holmes said, pulling one from its holster. "They're double-action, so you don't have to cock them before firing them—pulling the trigger does both. They break open like Doc's .44 Schofield, so they're easier and faster to reload than a Colt, but they fire .45 Colt cartridges. I sent my cousin in England a case of cartridges and he talked Philip Webley into designing revolvers to fire them. Now my cousin says Webley wants to sell pistols based on these to the British army but using a different cartridge. He's going to call his a .455, even though it's exactly the same caliber."

"Perhaps you would allow me to try one of them while you are in town?"

"It'd be my pleasure. But right now, Doc and I should be getting over to the Miller Hotel, so we can find out why we're here."

✗   ✗   ✗   ✗

"Let's get right to it," said Agent Robert Ross, a tall, fair-haired, clean-shaven man whose features were almost a parody of rugged handsomeness. "Representatives of our government and Mexico's are meeting at Fort Brown to negotiate a convention to solve a problem with the border between us and Mexico."

"What problem might that be?" Watson asked.

"The treaty that ended the Mexican-American War set the Rio Grande as the border in these parts. The problem is that whoever wrote up the treaty assumed that rivers always stay in the same place and the Rio Grande doesn't. The two sides are negotiating a convention that says what happens to the border whenever the river changes its course. My boss thinks someone wants to disrupt the negotiations. We need the two of you to help prevent that and to capture the parties responsible."

"That task would seem to be outside our mandate," Watson said. "Furthermore, our jurisdiction is Arizona, not Texas."

"Marshal Holmes has just been appointed a Special U.S. Marshal whose jurisdiction covers these entire United States. I have your copy of the appointment here," he said, handing an envelope to Holmes. "As his deputy, that goes for you as well, Dr. Watson, so you can both pin your badges back on now.

"As for your first objection," Ross continued, "we suspect that the parties involved may include Henry Judson Raymond or Fredericka Mandelbaum. Both are fugitives from justice and recapturing fugitives is clearly within the mandate of the U.S. Marshals Service."

"Speaking of mandates, how did you get mixed up in this?" Holmes asked. "Isn't the Secret Service the branch of the Treasury Department that tracks down counterfeiters?"

"That's what everyone is supposed to think. The truth is that we've been involved in a lot of different things over the years. In this case, our government fears the involvement of a European government and of a stateless person who doesn't recognize the authority of any government."

"You're real good at talking around the point," Holmes said, "but you might as well come right out and say that the European government you're talking about is the German Empire and the 'stateless person' is the former Prince Dakkar of Bundelkund, who calls himself Captain Nemo these days."

"But how did you know …?" Ross sputtered.

"Raymond was born in Germany as Adam Worth and Mandelbaum is from Prussia, so both have roots in the German Empire. And as for Captain Nemo, what other 'stateless person' could get the government so spooked?"

"But Captain Nemo is dead," Watson said.

"I've never believed that," Holmes said, "and obviously they don't believe it in Washington, either. He faked his death once; why not do it again? If everyone thinks that he's dead, nobody will be hunting for him." Holmes thought for a moment. "You know, there are some folks who call Raymond 'the Napoleon of Crime.' I would dearly love to see him behind bars."

⚹　⚹　⚹　⚹

After inspecting their hotel rooms, Holmes and Watson met in the lobby. They were immediately approached by a gray-haired gentleman with a weather-lined face and a rolling gait.

"You are Wyatt Holmes and Dr. John Watson, are you not?"

"We are," Watson said.

"Please allow me to introduce myself. I am Captain Henry Miller, the owner of this hotel. Would you do me the honor of being my guests for dinner?"

"We gratefully accept," Watson said.

"Thank you," Holmes said.

"Please come with me," Miller said. "I have a table prepared in the dining room."

Miller led them to a round table with four chairs arrayed around it, located in the corner of the room. By habit, Holmes and Watson seated themselves with their backs to the corner and Miller sat down beside Holmes.

"Shall I order for us?" Miller asked. Holmes and Watson nodded. Miller gestured to a waiter halfway across the room, held up three fingers and nodded. The waiter gave a shallow bow and turned towards the double doors leading to the kitchen.

"Impressive," Watson said.

"I gather that you're a sea captain and not an army captain?" Holmes asked Miller.

"Most observant, Marshal Holmes," Miller said. "You are entirely correct."

As they spoke, a party of five entered the dining room. In the lead was a portly, expensively-dressed man with a self-important demeanor, carrying a cane in one hand and a newspaper in the other. Following in his wake were two well-dressed men, also carrying newspapers. Behind them were a man who was trying unsuccessfully to look well-dressed and Agent Robert Ross of the Secret Service. The waiter gave the group a wide berth.

A tough-looking cowboy stood up to leave the dining room as the group entered. As he was about to pass the new arrivals, the portly man suddenly altered his course and jostled him. Taken unawares, the cowboy was knocked off balance. He spun around and fell face first across the table he just vacated. He stood up with the remains of his meal on his chest and murder in his eye.

"Turn around, you son of a …" he shouted, but Agent Ross moved between him and the portly man, his hand hovering over his pistol. The cowboy turned white. Without another word, he stalked out of the room.

"What in the Sam Hill was that all about?" Holmes asked his host.

"The fat, smug-looking 'gentleman' is Mr. J. Winston Duke, who has come from Washington as the U.S. government's chief negotiator for the border convention. What you have just seen is a little game he likes to play. He deliberately gives offence and lets his Secret Service protector deal with the consequences. During the first such incident, Agent Ross demonstrated how fast he is on the draw. Nobody has dared go up against him since."

"And the rest of the party?" Holmes asked.

"The taller of the two better-dressed men is Charles Pinder, Mr. Duke's secretary. The other, Roberto Alvarez, is here as a translator. Like Agent Ross, he is from Galveston. Although Mr. Alvarez is most proud of his Spanish heritage, he is very much a Texan— one of his grandfathers died defending the Alamo and the other was killed in the massacre at Goliad. The man in the ill-fitting suit is a local named Manuel Garcia. Another translator became severely ill and returned to Galveston, and Mr. Duke hired Garcia to take his place."

The group seated themselves at a nearby table. All but Garcia opened their menus.

"Excuse me," Holmes said as he got up and made for the door, motioning Ross to follow.

As soon as they were out of sight of the dining room, Holmes turned to Agent Ross. "Does he do that often?" he asked.

"Yes, but especially when he's having a bad day," Ross said. "He got a telegram this morning, and he's been in a foul mood ever since."

"He's a lowdown snake. How can you stand to work for him?"

"I have to agree with you, but protecting him is my job. Fortunately, that job is almost over. There was an unexpected breakthrough at the talks today and they finalized the provisions of the convention. The Mexican representatives are translating the document into Spanish this evening. All we have to do is check the wording tomorrow and I can take it to Washington to get it printed up and signed."

"They won't sign it here?" Holmes asked.

"No. I never met Duke before this assignment, but from what I've seen and heard he's a good negotiator. It's probably because underneath his smug, pompous exterior, he's an arrogant, self-centered son of a bitch. That said, people at his level don't sign international agreements. It will be signed in Washington, probably by Secretary of State Frelinghuysen and by Matías Romero, the Mexican envoy to the United States. Then it will be ratified by the presidents of both countries—at that point, a formality—and the convention will be made public."

"Well, it's a good thing Duke won't be around here much longer. He might rile someone who's faster on the draw than you are."

"Don't think it hasn't occurred to me," Ross said.

✗   ✗   ✗   ✗

The bushwhacking was planned for next morning and went off without a hitch.

As Duke, Pinder, Garcia, and Agent Ross entered the dining room, Watson intercepted Ross and steered him back into the lobby without attracting Duke's notice. Holmes, wearing a long coat, contrived to walk past the group as they trooped to the table they used the previous evening. As anticipated, Duke altered course in order to bump into the well-dressed stranger. Holmes anticipated this and compensated for it. The resulting collision saw Holmes keep his feet and Duke fall unceremoniously on his ample posterior. The newspaper Duke was carrying flew out of his hand and fluttered down to land on his head.

The enraged Duke turned to set Agent Ross on Holmes, but Ross was nowhere to be seen. Duke turned back to Holmes and, fist tightening on his cane, sized him up. Perhaps it was the breadth of Holmes's shoulders, or maybe it was the matched revolvers that became visible when Holmes swept back his coat; whatever the cause, Duke's demeanor changed so suddenly that Holmes nearly laughed out loud.

"Excuse me, sir, for jostling you," Duke said, his tone an amazing simulation of sincerity. "I must not have been watching where I was going. I most certainly did not mean to give offense."

"I accept your apology," Holmes said, matching Duke's feigned sincerity perfectly, "but you'd best be more careful while you're in these parts. There's lots of folks around here who might well take offense—deadly offense." And with that, Holmes returned to his table, to be joined by Watson.

A few minutes later, as Holmes and Watson surveyed the huge portions of food served by their grateful waiter, Duke put down his newspaper and rushed over to Holmes's table.

"Until just now, I did not realize you were the illustrious Wyatt Holmes. Please allow me to introduce myself. I am Winston Duke of the U.S. State Department."

"How do you do, sir," Holmes said, rising from his chair.

At that moment, Agent Ross strode up. "Gentlemen, could you come with me please? There is a … problem," Ross said.

Once in the lobby, Ross turned to Duke. "I checked on Mr. Alvarez to find out what was keeping him. His door was unlocked, and I found him in his room, dead. I've sent a bellboy to find the sheriff, but I'd like Marshal Holmes to take over the investigation, assuming you have no objection."

"I certainly have no objection," Duke said.

"Of course, Agent Ross," Holmes said. He looked through the dining room door, where Duke's secretary sat reading his paper and Garcia sat staring into space. Turning to Duke, he said, "You'll want to be the one to tell the others. We'll keep you up to date." Then he turned back to Agent Ross. "Why don't the three of us go on up and take a look?"

✗   ✗   ✗   ✗

"Well, at least he didn't die with his boots on. They're still outside his door," Holmes said.

"I'm a dentist, not a physician," Watson said as he examined the body, "but we can be quite certain that the cause of death is lead poisoning."

Ross was incredulous. "Lead poisoning?"

"That's Doc's way of being funny," Holmes said. "He means that Alvarez was shot. Probably one bullet through the heart, fired from the pistol lying on the floor under the sofa."

Ross knelt down and retrieved the weapon, which looked better suited to a child-sized pirate than an assassin. It was no more than six inches from end to end, with a rounded walnut stock, a caplock mechanism on its right side, and a short barrel with a sizeable bore.

"An old-style Philadelphia Deringer," Ross said, "like the one John Wilkes Booth used to shoot Abraham Lincoln. I wonder why no one heard the shot?"

"There's powder burns on that sofa cushion," Holmes said. "Whoever did this used it to deaden the sound."

"Obviously this is an attempt to disrupt the conference, so we're probably dealing with Henry Judson Raymond," Ross said. "He couldn't have known that the negotiations are complete and that killing Alvarez gained him nothing."

"Watson and I will wait here for Sheriff Brito," Holmes said. "You might as well go tell Mr. Duke to get on with things. There's a private banquet room off the dining room. When you're done for the day, bring everyone straight there. Don't let them go back to their rooms first."

As Ross left the room, Holmes took up a newspaper from the end table next to the sofa and handed it to Watson. "We may as well read the *Daily Cosmopolitan* while we're waiting."

"Why would you want to do that?" Sheriff Brito said as he entered the room, followed by his two deputies.

"Well, now that you're here we've got better things to do," Holmes said. "I'd be obliged if one of your deputies could stay here and keep an eye on things. Have the other one hunt down Captain Miller for us. Doc, I need you to go to the telegraph office and then meet us at the courthouse. There's a lot of things we've got to get done if we're going to finish this up today."

"What are those two doing here?" Winston Duke asked as his party filed into the banquet room.

"They're here because I want them here," Holmes said. "There was a murder today, so it should be pretty plain why Sheriff Brito is here, and Captain Miller has information that bears on this case. Any objections?"

Holmes stared Duke down before he continued.

"Now the three things you have to know to solve any crime are means, motive, and opportunity. In this case, the means was the pistol on the table here. The assassin left it behind in Mr. Alvarez's hotel room because he didn't want to take the chance that someone might find it on him. It's the sign of a professional criminal.

"The opportunity is straightforward as well. The assassin got into Mr. Alvarez's room without breaking the door down, so either he picked the lock or Alvarez knew the assassin and let him in. Then he drew the Deringer with one hand, picked up the sofa cushion with the other, and used the cushion to muffle the sound of the shot.

"That brings us to motive. Alvarez was one of two translators sent from Galveston. The other one got sick and went home a week back, which took him out of the negotiations. This murder has taken Alvarez out of the negotiations, too, just in a different way."

"What are you getting at, Holmes?" Agent Ross asked.

"After the other translator left, Mr. Duke hired Mr. Garcia here to take his place. Now he probably talks good English and Spanish, but I'm thinking there's something he can't do. Last night at dinner everyone else at his table was reading their menus except him. This morning at breakfast, Mr. Pinder was reading a newspaper, but Mr. Garcia was just sitting there doing nothing, even though there was a newspaper right beside him. Unless I'm wrong, Mr. Garcia here can't read. Isn't that right, Mr. Garcia?"

Garcia stared at the table and nodded.

"This means that Mr. Alvarez was the only translator who could have read the Spanish version of the border convention this morning. Agent Ross, do you have it with you?"

Ross opened a dispatch case and pulled out a thin sheaf of papers bound together by a ribbon.

"Sheriff Brito puts out the local Spanish-language newspaper, so his Spanish must be good. I'd like him to go over that document."

"I must object ..." Duke began.

"And I must insist," Holmes said.

Ross shrugged and handed the document to Brito. It took him only a few minutes to read both texts from end to end. Then he turned back to the middle of the document and studied a few paragraphs with great care.

"This is an interesting translation," Brito said at last. "The English text states that the border between the United States and Mexico lies in the center of the normal channel of the Rio Grande, even if minor changes to the course of that channel should occur through natural means. However, if there is a major change, either by natural or artificial means, the border will remain where the channel was when a survey was done in 1852. There is a subtle difference in the Spanish text. In the case of a major change to the course of the channel, this wording allows the Mexican government to accept the new channel as its border."

"That's pretty much what I suspected," Holmes said. "Think about it. If someone changes the course of the Rio Grande southward—and it wouldn't take much dynamite to do it—the American border would remain where it is, but the Mexican government could accept the new channel as its border. That would leave a no-man's-land in the middle. Captain Miller, what can you tell us about the land directly south of the Rio Grande between here and the Gulf of Mexico? Who lives there?"

"It's mostly sand dunes and swampland," Miller said, "only a few feet above sea level, except for a narrow strip along the coast. Not many people live there any more. Most who remain are the last of an unfortunate group of former Texans of German ancestry. Because they supported the Union, the Confederates hunted them during the Civil War. They fled across the Rio Grande to a place called Bagdad, at the mouth of the river, but the Mexican government allowed Confederate soldiers to cross the border and hunt them. The Union took so long to send a ship to rescue them that they felt abandoned. A handful remained in Bagdad and a handful of others returned there after the war, because there was nothing left for them in Texas.

"Bagdad was an important port during the Civil War, but only because it was both accessible to the Confederacy and immune to the Union blockade. The Confederates shipped out cotton and received armaments in return and there was nothing that the Union could do about it.

"As a port, though, Bagdad was sadly lacking because the water is too shallow for ocean-going ships to dock there. They were forced to anchor in the Gulf of Mexico, half a cable offshore, and transfer cargoes back and forth in small, flat-bottomed steamboats and barges. Also, the town was in an exposed position and was devastated by every big storm that came through here. Officially, the town does not even exist any more, but some still live there and eke out a living from those few ships that still choose to transfer cargoes there."

"Let's suppose," Holmes said, "that you asked these people to choose which country they wanted to belong to. How would they vote?"

"I have no idea. The South persecuted them, Mexico allowed it to happen, and for far too long the North did nothing to help them. They have no great love for either country."

"Now supposing they could become part of a whole other country, let's say the German Empire?"

"They would almost certainly jump at the chance."

"Preposterous!" Duke said.

"Not if you think about it. The Germans badly want a coaling station in the Caribbean for their navy. They'd be happy to build a harbor out of nothing if they could get hold of a place to build it. We wouldn't lose any territory, so we wouldn't really have anything to complain about. I know all about the Monroe Doctrine, but you'll remember that we didn't do much when France installed Maximilian as Emperor of Mexico twenty years back. Do you think President Arthur could sell folks on going to war with Germany over a few square miles of Mexican swampland?"

"And what about Mexico?" Ross asked.

Holmes shrugged. "Porfirio Díaz may not be president down there any more, but he's still running the show. You remember what he said? 'Poor Mexico, so far from God and so close to the United States.' There's nothing he'd like better than to stick a fork in Uncle Sam's eye. Besides, the Germans would probably let Mexico share their fancy new harbor."

"Matías Romero would never be party to such a thing!" Duke said.

"Romero and Díaz have a friendship of long standing," Brito said, "and Díaz is married to Romero's daughter. I cannot think that Romero would go against Díaz's wishes in anything."

"Now we're getting to the motive," Holmes said. "This little scheme could only work if the tricky Spanish wording of the convention went unnoticed. Since Mr. Garcia can't read, he wouldn't pick up on it, but Alvarez was sure to. If the talks went on for as long as they were supposed to, maybe Alvarez might have taken sick like the other translator. But when the talks ended all of a sudden there wasn't time to get rid of Alvarez any other way but to kill him."

"So did Henry Raymond do this or not?" Ross asked.

"Keep your shirt on for just a little longer," Holmes said. "I wondered about the telegram that you told me about, the one that put Mr. Duke in such a bad mood, so I sent Doc to talk to the telegraph clerk. According to him, the telegram said that another translator was being sent here from Galveston and should arrive the day after tomorrow. That's why the agreement happened all of a sudden—so everything could be concluded before the new translator got here.

"And then there was the newspaper in Alvarez's room. It was the *Daily Cosmopolitan*. I thought it was funny that Alvarez would want to read an English-language newspaper when there's such a good Spanish-language paper in town, so I asked Captain Miller about it. He told me that Alvarez was getting *El Demócrata* delivered to his room every morning. I figure the assassin was carrying the *Daily Cosmopolitan* when he came into the room. He put down the newspaper so he could pick up the sofa cushion. He shot Alvarez, dropped the pistol and the sofa cushion and then picked up the wrong newspaper before he left the room. When I was eating breakfast this morning, Mr. Duke here came up and introduced himself. The only way he could have recognized me was from my picture in the paper he was reading. Sheriff Brito told me when we first got here that the English-language papers don't have my likeness, which meant Mr. Duke was reading *El Demócrata*.

That didn't seem right to me either, so I asked Captain Miller. Sure enough, Mr. Duke was getting the *Daily Cosmopolitan.*"

"This is meaningless nonsense!" Duke said.

"That may be, but when Sheriff Brito, Captain Miller, and I went to the courthouse this morning, the justice of the peace thought it meant enough to give me a search warrant for your hotel room. We found two very interesting things hidden in your luggage."

Holmes took a small bottle out of his pocket and set it on the table. "Doc figures this would make someone sick if it was slipped into his food or drink over a period of a few days. We'll have it checked out just to be sure. Still, this is just something extra. Here's the real prize."

Holmes reached back into his pocket, removed a Deringer and set it on the table.

"Deringer almost always sold his pistols in pairs," Holmes said, "so I was counting on finding this. You can see plain as day that it's the twin of the one that killed Alvarez."

"All of this proves nothing," Duke said. "When I get back to Washington I shall have you removed from your appointment."

"You won't be going back to Washington because you never came from Washington. I believe you're really Adam Worth, also known as Henry Judson Raymond."

"Preposterous!" Duke said. "Mr. Pinder will vouch for my identity."

"I'm sure he will," Holmes said, "but there's one more thing. When you left Alvarez's room, you needed to be sure that no one saw you. You needed a lookout waiting outside the door to tell you when the coast was clear. That accomplice was Mr. Pinder here, who I'm thinking is really your old friend Charlie Bullard. Bullard is a safecracker, so he could have unlocked the door to Mr. Alvarez's room for you.

"I reckon you two got on the same ship that the real Duke and Pinder took to get here from Galveston. Somewhere along the way you dry-gulched them and threw them overboard. Nobody here knew Duke and Pinder, so impersonating them wasn't a problem. While Doc was at the telegraph office he sent a telegram to Washington asking for your descriptions. We should get the answer in the morning and that should settle who you really are. For now, though, the two of you are under arrest for the murder of Roberto Alvarez. Sheriff Brito, they're all yours."

Brito whistled sharply. His two deputies came into the room with pistols drawn, took charge of the prisoners and bundled them out the door.

"And now," Holmes said, "I figure we all deserve a good meal."

"Great idea," Agent Ross said. "The State Department is buying."

Shortly after they ordered their meals, Brito's deputies staggered into the room. "They jumped us," one of them said, "maybe six of them, all wearing funny-looking sailor-type uniforms. They dragged us across the river to Mexico with them on the ferry. There were two more sailors waiting there, with enough horses for all of them. They let us go and lit out, riding east."

"They are probably heading for Bagdad," Brito said. "They'll have to swing south, below the bend in the Rio Grande, and then ride northeast. We can go straight down the Boca Chica road for most of the way and perhaps reach the mouth of the river before they do."

"Doc, let's you and me get our rifles. Sheriff, can you round up half a dozen horses? Deputy, send a telegram to Port Isabel. Tell them to form a posse and head south in a steamboat. Maybe we can get them back."

"But they'll be sure to stay in either Mexican or international waters," Ross objected.

"As long as we can get them into a courtroom," Holmes said, "the judge won't care how they got there."

✗　✗　✗　✗

Their vantage point was only a dozen feet above the waves, little more than a sand dune anchored tenuously in place by a scattering of grass and scrub. Still, it was the highest ground available. Two hundred yards offshore, the full moon illuminated a large boat whose eight rowers were fighting the wind to move farther out into the Gulf of Mexico, urged on by a helmsman and two passengers. The steamboat from Port Isabel was nowhere in sight. Ross, Brito, and the two deputies looked on helplessly.

"Gentlemen, I'd like you to meet Josephine," Holmes said as he pulled his rifle out of its fringed leather case. "She's a Purdey .470

caliber side-by-side express rifle with a telescopic sight by William Malcolm. Let's see if she can slow that rowboat down some."

Holmes lay down on his stomach and rested Josephine's forestock on the top of the dune. As he was taking aim, a large black object rose from the water, blocking the line of sight to his target.

"What on earth?" Watson asked. "Is that … the *Nautilus*?"

"Well, that's that," Holmes said. "Even Josephine won't be able to hurt that thing."

The *Nautilus* remained in view for a few minutes. Then a powerful light illuminated the ocean ahead of the legendary craft as it slipped gracefully beneath the waves. It left behind the boat, which now held two men rowing awkwardly toward shore.

"I reckon those two clumsy oarsmen are the real Winston Duke and Charles Pinder," Holmes said.

✗   ✗   ✗   ✗

"So Captain Nemo rescued you after Raymond and Bullard threw you overboard?" Holmes asked.

"You are entirely correct," Duke said, still out of breath from his exertions, "and moreover, he was a gracious host. Indeed, for an imprisonment it was a most agreeable experience."

"How did he get involved in this, anyway?"

"He needed a component for the *Nautilus* that was beyond his resources to manufacture. The only thing he insisted on was that there be no taking of life. That is why he followed our ship and pulled us out of the Gulf of Mexico." Duke turned to Ross. "You will have to inform the Mexican delegation that negotiations will resume tomorrow."

"You aren't going to wait for the new translator?" Ross asked.

"I have asked Sheriff Brito to fill that role for the time being," Duke said.

"It's too bad that Raymond and Bullard will escape unpunished, though," Watson said.

"I wouldn't count on that," Pinder said. "Nemo's men told him about Raymond and Bullard murdering Alvarez and he went into a towering rage. I believe he intends to have them marooned."

"This Nemo might not be the evil monster everyone makes him out to be," Watson said.

Holmes nodded in agreement. "It looks like there's nothing left to do except head back to the Miller Hotel and the fine meal that Mr. Duke here is buying us."

Jim Robb is an accountant working as the controller of a multinational jewelry company. A former army reserve officer, he is a life member of the Royal Canadian Armoured Corps Association (Cavalry). Jim and his wife Donna live in southern Saskatchewan, Canada with their canine and feline associates.

THE RED HERRING LEAGUE

by Bradley Harper

25 October, 1991

TO: Lloyd Baxter, Esq
        Baxter and Associates, LLC
        495 Pall Mall, London

FROM: Henrietta Wilson
        Associate Bank Manager
        Lloyd's Banking Group
        3609 Regents Street, London

Sir,

The following correspondence was discovered when a safe deposit box with a one-hundred-year deposit was opened upon the expiration of said deposit. As your firm originally established the account, I have forwarded it to you in hopes you may find a legal recipient.

If you are unable to find anyone entitled to it, as a member of the Board of Directors of the Victoria and Albert Museum, we would gladly accept this message from Sherlock Holmes's arch nemesis Professor Moriarty. This recounting of his first encounter with Holmes, composed while *en route* to his final and fatal rendezvous with him at the Reichenbach Falls, is a priceless piece of British history. Be assured we would proudly display his version of their first meeting with the public, which would grant the Professor's wish that his voice be heard beyond the grave.

Respectfully,
HW

15 April, 1891
Special train, *en route* to Lucerne

Jonathon Hopkins, Esq
495 Pall Mall
London

Mister Hopkins,

This will probably be the final letter you receive from me. Whether or no, I suspect your services as my solicitor are at an end. My final instructions regarding the disposition of my earthly effects are already in your custody. I ask you to enclose the attached letter into my safe deposit box, with instructions it not be opened for one hundred years. I should like for it to be posted as a Letter to the Editor of *The Times*, as my rebuttal to Doctor Watson's slavish depiction of his companion, Sherlock Holmes.

A century should be long enough that no shame may accrue to my long-deceased relations, but short enough that my name may still be remembered. As I have no doting Watson to tell my side of our encounter and neither publisher nor public to please, it falls to me to tell the true version of events.

I thank you for your loyal service. You will find your final remittance in the safe deposit box in an envelope addressed to you.

If I survive the following week, I shall, however, require the services of a more-than-competent barrister. We shall discuss that requirement when or if I find myself returned to London.

In closing, Sir, I would advise you to choose your friends with care, but your enemies even more so.

Respectfully,
Professor James Moriarty

15 April, 1891

To the Citizens of the Twentieth Century,

As I pursue the man who has destroyed everything I have laboured decades to achieve, I still marvel that my first encounter with Sherlock Holmes was scarcely six months ago. I had heard of the difficulties he was causing various of my competitors and

I admit to a flagrant case of *Schadenfreude*, the unseemly enjoyment of the suffering of others. I bore Mister Holmes no ill will at the time, the enemy of my enemy … you understand. My feelings towards him changed, however, after his intrusion into my own affairs—starting with that deuced case of the Red-Headed League.

It was the ninth of October, 1890, when I inspected the tunnel in the basement of the pawnshop after John Clay informed me he was two days from entering the vault of the City and Suburban Bank. I was only recently ensconced as the head of the London criminal underworld. I therefore saw this project as my opportunity to cement my position and earn the respect of even the most disreputable members of British Society.

John Clay was one of my more capable lieutenants and I had great plans for him. Putting him in charge of this undertaking was a means for me to advance his experience and thus usefulness to me. A man of impeccable breeding, he could be an insufferable boor at times. Fortunately, as we are of the same social class, he tolerated my instructions with little outward dissent.

Everything seemed as it should. The imbecile pawnbroker Jabez Wilson's greed was matched only by the bright hue of his red hair and so was easily distracted into the absurd task of copying the *Encyclopedia Britannica* at the rate of four pounds a week. Clay's improvisation of the Red Headed League to get Wilson out of the way while the tunnel was constructed, is evidence my faith in him was well-founded. I felt I had taken everything into consideration and my calculations felt as secure as any differential equation of calculus.

Regretfully, I left two things out of my formula: the extent of Wilson's greed, and Sherlock Holmes.

Never one to leave things to chance, I queried my "consultants" within the Metropolitan Police Force, to see if any rumour reached them of our intended pillage of the bank. There really is no honour among thieves and a miscreant caught for one offence, is quick to tell of another's in hopes of lessening his own punishment. Men will talk in their cups or to their wives or lovers (or both). Given the size of the fortune that awaited us on the far side of the vault walls—thirty thousand pounds worth of gold "Napoleons" on loan from the Bank of France—I wanted no last-minute alarms.

Assured all was well, I decided to accompany my rogues that fateful night. I did so partly to bolster their morale, partly to savour the victory with them and to ensure the spoils were accurately accounted for. I am a cautious man by nature, so despite my expectation that the night would go exactly as I planned, I "took precautions," though not in the way Doctor Watson is known to do while accompanying Holmes on one of his lurid escapades.

I was as excited as a bride on her wedding day. The funds awaiting me would do much to extend my network of informers and the acclaim I would earn for this bold venture would bring many new allies to my organization. I shivered in the cool, dank basement, whether from the autumn chill or my anticipation and savoured the smell of the freshly-turned earth. It was the smell of success.

I hung back as my second man, Archie, swung the pickaxe the final few times. John Clay went forward into the darkness with Archie close behind while I listened for any alarm from the darkness ahead or above.

I was about to enter the vault when a lantern flared and I heard Clay exclaim, "Jump, Archie, jump and I'll swing for it!"

Then an arrogant voice stated calmly, "It's no use, John Clay. You have no chance at all." I did not know it yet, but I had just heard the voice of that accursed Holmes for the first time.

Archie, fortunately for me, ran back into the basement and up the stairs as fast as he could, but as he reached the landing I heard the entrance of the pawnshop above crash open. Archie's abrupt appearance threw the bobbies off balance for just a moment, giving me a chance to step into the shadows. I knew the gaping hole into the bank vault would draw the eyes of the excited constables so that they would not search the basement thoroughly right away.

A police inspector with Archie in tow kept his wits about him, but as one bobby raced through the opening. I, attired as a police constable, closely followed. In the poor light of the vault, one more uniformed figure, face poorly discernible by the light of a bull's eye lantern, was indistinguishable from his fellows. With the other bobby remaining in the pawnshop basement, the number of bobbies on each side of the opening seemed appropriate.

In the dark I had the leisure to study Mister Holmes and his sycophant Doctor Watson at close range. In his narratives in *The Strand*, Watson portrays Holmes as dismissive of any fame he might earn as a detective. A load of rubbish to make the man appear more agreeable. In truth, I found him quite boastful and arrogant. In other circumstances, he and John Clay would be fitting companions.

Holmes and Clay exchanged compliments, as though they had just completed a game of tennis and I found their attempts to out-flatter the other most irritating. To them it was but a contest to see who was the cleverer, while I fumed in the dark, sorely missing the vast sum which had just eluded my grasp.

Others have remarked upon the similarities in appearance between Holmes and myself. In the dark, it was difficult to appraise facial features. I can only say that we are taller than average, slender and more intelligent than the vast majority of humanity. That he uses his gifts to bring ruin upon me appears monstrous, especially as I contemplate what a splendid partnership we could have forged.

I learned later of Holmes's older brother who was generally perceived as being even more intelligent, so I believe he is driven by a child-like need to exceed his sibling. Such deep-rooted needs can lead to obsession and madness, to be sure, but are often the hallmarks of greatness as well. In Holmes's case, I feel the two are inextricable.

Once Clay and Holmes finished preening in front of one another, I was directed by the inspector within the vault to lead Master Clay to the waiting police wagon. Clay's eyes and mine met for an instant, but he proved my trust in him and kept mum. He knew I would spare no expense in his defense, as did Archie, who was already in the wagon when I, along with two real constables, rejoined them. As no funds were lost by the bank, prosecution would not be overly vigorous. I knew whose ear to whisper into and whose palm to grease to ensure my thieves would get the best defense and poorest prosecution possible.

I told the bobbies I would report back to Inspector Jones, still in the vault, then slipped away into the darkness. I confess to some small satisfaction that no one noticed an extra constable at the scene. Uniforms have proven a useful means to turn invisible before and since.

It was a bitter loss, but in my profession the cost of doing business. In hindsight, my ability to offer some protection to my men strengthened my credibility among the criminal class and the loyalty of my henchmen. My personal reputation was also enhanced as the tale of my walking among the constabulary and beneath the very nose of Sherlock Holmes, only to stroll freely away, was shared within the criminal underworld. A master mariner learns to turn every wind to his advantage. Thus my maiden encounter with Mr Holmes would appear at first blush to have been a resounding victory for him. I am proud to say that I eked out a stalemate, which was all the sweeter as he was unaware of how I turned this setback to my advantage.

Sadly, I am not always so skillful or he was more so. In any event, our growing animosity will soon reach its climax. The sight of the Alps announces my imminent arrival in Lucerne, where my associate will post this letter to my retainer. Then I will use Colonel Moran's skill as a hunter to drive my quarry to ground and exact a reckoning for all the damage he has caused me. I trust this narrative may serve as a "message in a bottle," revealing the true story of our duel of wits, when the Earthly Statute of Limitations is long past and our bones turned to dust.

Will our names outlive us, I wonder? If I am linked to his demise, then Holmes will have done me a favour I can never repay and this time I may have to award *him* a stalemate.

Until?
Professor James Moriarty

Bradley Harper is a prior US Army pathologist who began writing shortly after retirement. His first novel, *A Knife in the Fog*, comes out October 2 and involves a young Arthur Conan Doyle in the hunt for Jack the Ripper, until the Ripper starts stalking him!

THE ADVENTURE OF THE GOLDEN LOCKS

by Ed DeJesus

As Holmes and I passed through the woods, we suddenly came upon a rather broad clearing in which stood a most charming small cottage. I began to approach the front door, but Holmes stopped me with a gesture.

"I pray you stand away from the door, Watson," said he. "We may find some foot-marks that may aid us in our investigation."

I did as he requested and he immediately threw himself onto the lawn and scrutinized the ground minutely with his glass. After a few moments he motioned me to approach closer and indicated the grassy area and path near the door.

"You see, Watson, that there are four distinct sets of foot-marks. Three sets lead away from the door to the side and across the lawn. All three of these sets were made by bears, one evidently very large and probably male, another middle-sized and female and the third undoubtedly a baby bear of indeterminate gender. Their tracks lead toward the forest."

He pointed toward the ground once more. "The final set of foot-marks is very different, however. These lead toward the door, rather than away from it and as you can no doubt observe, overlay the other tracks in no less than two places, showing that this person entered the house some time after the bears left it. For it was a person, Watson. Probably also a child and unless I am greatly mistaken, a girl."

At this Holmes bounded forward and examined the frame of the door with his lens and presently gave a cry of discovery. "Look here, Watson! A single strand of hair. Blond and so consequently not from one of the bears. Long, therefore from a female. And from its position so low on the door-frame, evidently from a child. A perfect confirmation of our surmises about the footmarks. She must have thrust her head through the partially-opened door to look inside, suggesting that she did not belong in the house and was surveying the interior before entering."

Attempting to imitate my more capable friend, I bent to examine the lock. "Holmes, I see no signs that the lock was picked," said I. "In addition, there are no marks on the jamb. I would guess that this door was left open deliberately."

"Excellent, Watson," Holmes said, nodding sharply. "I concur completely."

Holmes stepped up to the door and pushed it slowly inward. Seeing no one within, we entered what was obviously the kitchen of the cottage. A wooden slab table was flanked by two benches. On the tabletop stood three thick porcelain bowls with spoons beside each bowl and crude rustic mugs. The two larger bowls held some type of hot cereal, while the smallest held only the residue of the same cereal. Holmes sniffed at one of the bowls.

"Porridge," he pronounced. "A large bowl for the large bear, a medium bowl for the female and a small bowl for the cub."

"But Holmes, why should they leave their breakfast and go off into the forest?"

Holmes narrowed his gaze and then placed his hand on each of the bowls in turn. "This large bowl is only now cool enough to eat. At the time that the bears left, I surmise that all the bowls must have been too hot. No doubt the walk was undertaken in order to allow their breakfast to cool."

"And the empty bowl?"

Holmes gave a slight smile. "Since at the time of her visit the porridge must have been just right, I think that must be the work of our small visitor. As is that broken chair."

I turned abruptly to view what he was describing. A small parlor opened off the kitchen. It was sparsely furnished with but three chairs. One of these was large and stiff and another was a soft easy chair. But what was most apparent was that a child's wooden chair lay in pieces in one area by itself. The sight was so startling that I gave a short exclamation as I noticed it.

Holmes's smile grew broader. "Our little friend is clearly larger than the cub and not so graceful. Now given that our burglar with the golden curls entered and has not left, yet is nowhere to be seen, where might she have concealed herself?"

He cast his eyes about the room and then intensified his gaze. I followed his look and noticed, for the first time, a stairway that led from the far end of the parlor. Touching his forefinger to his lips, Holmes stole forward on tiptoe, careful to place his feet on the carpeting of the room and while passing up the stairway itself, on the runner at the center of each step.

Thus we crept upstairs until we gained a large and well-lit bed-chamber. Immediately by the stair-head was a very large bed. Holmes pressed his hand upon the covers and shook his head in dismissal. I followed his example and found that this bed was too hard for all but the most sound sleeper. A second, middle-sized bed we examined likewise, finding it exceedingly and unpleasantly too soft.

Holmes suddenly held one hand aloft and at the same instant I became aware of a drowsy sigh proceeding from yet another bed in the room. This one was smaller than the other two. From our angle of approach, it was impossible to see who or what occupied this bed. Holmes stepped sideways stealthily, then cocked his head to one side as he surveyed the scene. When I drew up beside him, I saw what so arrested his attention.

A young girl perhaps eight or nine years old lay asleep on the bed. Her head with the golden curls that Holmes anticipated rested upon the soft white pillow, while her frame sprawled in the innocently awkward repose of childhood slumber on the coverlet.

From long experience, I knew Holmes to be devoid of the tender emotions so alien to his precise and analytical nature. Yet as he contemplated the sleeping child, I beheld on his face an expression of such kindly and gentle regard that I could almost believe that I were looking at the girl's own dear father rather than the renowned sleuth-hound of the law.

At this moment the sound of pawsteps from downstairs, accompanied by muffled voices, told us that the ursine residents of the cottage had returned home. The girl started up from her sleep at the noises and cast anxious glances at Holmes and myself.

Holmes extended a calming hand and addressed her in low tones. "I pray you not discommode yourself, young lady. I am Mr. Sherlock Holmes and this is my friend and colleague Dr. John Watson." I bowed at the introduction. "We shall be happy to act for you in this circumstance, Miss—"

"Goldilocks," replied the young girl, sitting up.

"Of course," Holmes murmured. "I should have guessed. And now I believe we are about to meet our hosts."

During his brief interview with the young lady we heard snatches of conversation from downstairs as the bears discovered, in turn, the emptied bowl of porridge and the broken chair. The tones of their outrage were unmistakable. We now perceived their rapid footfalls as they ascended the staircase.

I was glad at that moment that we were present to assist Goldilocks in her encounter with the bears. Regardless of the equivocal position that she found herself in as an uninvited occupant of their home, I have no doubt that their sudden arrival and fearsome appearance would have frightened her most severely had not Holmes and I quickly interposed ourselves.

"Ah," said Holmes, as they stood glowering with anger about their bed-chamber. "I believe I have the honor of addressing Papa Bear, Mama Bear and Baby Bear."

They stared at him but made no reply. Holmes rapidly introduced us all, at which Papa Bear lumbered across the room and gesticulated violently.

"What are you doing in our house?" he demanded gruffly.

"As to the manner of entry," Holmes continued, "I believe that Miss Goldilocks made her way here with the intention of paying you a social call. However, finding no one at home and your door ajar, she undertook to await your presence. We, in turn, were merely following her."

Vexed and unmollified, Papa Bear bellowed, "She ate our porridge!"

Holmes gave a brief nod and said, "This is true. However, I submit that, had she not done so, the porridge would have become too cold for consumption by the time of your arrival and you would have been obliged to dispose of it in any event."

At this Mama Bear declared, "She broke our chair!"

Holmes smiled. "That a guest should seek to sit in a chair is not an outrageous act. That the selected chair should not be capable of accommodating her frame is certainly not the fault of the young lady."

"But she's sleeping in my bed!" exclaimed Baby Bear.

"For which rest and repose she is, I am sure, immensely grateful," Holmes replied. "And now I believe that we shall accompany our client to her home, where, I have no doubt, her presence will have been missed by this time. I bid you good day."

With something of a flourish, he guided Goldilocks from the room. I still recall the looks of bafflement upon the faces of the three bears as we left them.

During the brief walk to the home of the young lady, Holmes remarked, "A not uninstructive case, Watson. In certain features it rather resembles another adventure in the forest that you were kind enough to record for me."

"Assuredly, Holmes," I agreed heartily. "The case involving that wolf and the trio of diminutive pigs."

✗

Ed DeJesus lives in the Boston area with his wife and family. He has published short stories in *Alfred Hitchcock's Mystery Magazine*, *The Leading Edge*, *Café Irreal*, *Fables*, and *Lunch Reads*. He has also self-published two mystery novels (*The Law of Falling Bodies* and *A Body in Motion*).

SHERLOCK HOLMES AND THE AMERICAN ASSASSIN

by T. J. Guiney

In the spring of 1902, Holmes and I had been in St Paul, Minnesota, helping our friend Shadwell Rafferty. The case was one of embezzlement, that threatened to bring down the Governor and his entire coalition in the ruling Democratic party. With the public screaming for impeachment, Holmes and I had been able to prove that the Governor was blameless and that the perpetrator was actually a low-level functionary in the opposition party. The Governor was exonerated, and Rafferty went back to his role as a saloonkeeper, with a bit of private detection on the side.

Holmes and I were now headed east. We had boarded a Northern Pacific sleeper in Minneapolis bound for Chicago, and then changed to a Southern Pacific to Boston via Albany, New York. We were rattling through Pennsylvania near Scranton, soon to cross into upstate New York. Holmes was in the window seat gazing out at the passing cityscape. He had been quiet for more than an hour. He was pensive, seemingly lost in thought. He would often retire into the recesses of his remarkable brain, rehashing one or another aspect of a case. I presumed that he was now ruminating about the problem that we solved in St Paul.

Our quiet reverie was interrupted by the appearance of a train porter who walked briskly by the glass door to our private compartment and then abruptly stopped, turned, and knocked on our door.

He entered and said, "Is one of you gentlemen Sherlock Holmes?"

Holmes looked at me in surprise and said, "I'm Sherlock Holmes."

The fellow seemed a bit shaken to be in the presence of the great detective. He collected himself and said: "Mr Holmes, the conductor has received a message via radio for you. It is requested by one Shadwell Rafferty that you detrain in Springfield, Massachusetts. We will be approaching Springfield in fifty-five minutes. You will be met at the station by a Mr Finbar Rafferty, who will explain. The message is marked URGENT."

"Thank you, young man" said Holmes.

I fished in the pocket of my waistcoat and found an American ten cent piece and handed it to the porter. He thanked me, turned and left us, closing the door to our compartment.

"What could this be about, Holmes?"

"Certainly nothing having to do with the Minnesota business. I expect that it has something to do with Rafferty's brother."

"Shad spoke to me once about his brother," I said. "I have a recollection that the brother is a politician in Springfield. Reasonably high up in the Mayor's office."

"We'll find out soon enough," said Holmes. He then closed his eyes and leaned his head back on the padded bench. He drifted off to sleep.

In exactly fifty-four minutes the porter was back, knocking on the door of our compartment. He popped his head in and said: "Mr Holmes, we're just coming into Union Station in Springfield, Massachusetts. Your trunks are at the door. It's been a pleasure having you gentlemen aboard. We wish you a pleasant stay in Springfield."

We emerged out onto the platform in the early afternoon sun, stretched our limbs after the long trip on the rails, and saw a huge man approaching us with a gaggle of assistants.

"Mr Holmes. Dr Watson. Thank God you got my message. I'm Finbar Rafferty." He shoved his enormous right hand toward us and proceeded with a muscle-cringing hand shake.

"It is a pleasure to meet you, Finbar," I said. "Your brother has become quite a dear friend over the years."

"So I understand. Please call me Finn, gentlemen."

"We're happy to be here, Finn, and to be of whatever service we might offer," replied my companion.

"Marvelous. Follow me, gentlemen. I have a carriage waiting outside the station to take us immediately to City Hall. There we can brief you on the emergency that we're facing. The carriage will take your trunks to the Massasoit Hotel on Main Street. I've reserved a suite of rooms for you there."

The carriage pulled up behind the massive structure that was Springfield City Hall. We were quickly shuffled in behind Rafferty and up the grand stairway to the Mayor's office on the fourth level. Rafferty knocked twice, and we were ushered in. We walked through an ante-room and proceeded through a polished mahogany double door into the Mayor's private office. The Mayor was sitting behind his desk. He took off his glasses and stood to greet us.

"Mr Mayor," said Rafferty, "allow me to introduce Mr Sherlock Holmes and Dr John Watson. Gentlemen, this is Mayor Thomas Kenneally."

Holmes spoke first. "Pleased to make your acquaintance, Mr Mayor," he said, and proffered his hand.

I followed suit with a similar greeting and accepted the Mayor's hand.

"I can't tell you how grateful I am that you have interrupted your journey to help our city deal with something very insidious," said Kenneally. "We have a dire emergency on our hands."

"Mr Mayor, we're pleased to be here and to assist you in any way that we can. Since time appears to be short, please tell us about the situation in careful detail. Don't leave anything out," said Holmes, taking a seat in front of the Mayor's grand desk. I joined him in the second chair.

"Let me begin at the beginning," said Mayor Kenneally. "There is a conference and large celebratory dinner scheduled to take place in Springfield at the Massasoit Hotel in two days. It is the tenth anniversary of the founding of the Sierra Club, and the club is honouring its two founders—the Scotsman John Muir and our new President, Theodore Roosevelt, who succeeded President McKinley after he was assassinated in Buffalo less than a year ago. Springfield is a small city and we're not accustomed to hosting affairs involving the sitting President of the United States. There is a great deal of anxiety across the city, the more so due to the fact that McKinley was assassinated by the Polish anarchist Leon Czolgosz. Now with Roosevelt on the way, our police force will be looking for anarchists around every street corner."

"I understand the heightened concern," said Holmes. "I'd expect such under the circumstances. But I'm sure the President will have extra security when he travels. But how does the anarchist hysteria, if I might call it that, affect Watson and me?"

"My office received this letter two days ago. It is unsigned, and it was mailed from a post box in downtown Springfield." He pushed a soiled envelope across to Holmes.

Holmes opened the envelope and read the small folded letter without any reaction. He studied it for several seconds without comment.

"What does it say, Holmes?" I said.

"It says: *Prepare. Rosevelt will be executed in Springfield.* Roosevelt is misspelled."

"Good God!" I uttered. "Do you think it's a serious threat?"

"If we didn't think that it's a serious threat, we wouldn't have interrupted your trip to Boston," replied Kenneally.

"Did the assassin in Buffalo give any such advance warning?" asked Holmes. "Any letter or telegram? Anything to alert the authorities in advance?"

"Nothing that we are aware of," piped in Rafferty, joining the conversation.

"I'm not surprised," said Holmes. "Although I haven't studied assassination attempts by anarchists very thoroughly, I have a strong feeling that anarchists take credit after the deed is done, rather than offering a warning in advance, because the outcome is of utmost importance to the assassination plot. On the other hand, angry people with a grudge or crazy people on some imagined mission to right a wrong, tend to send messages like this one. They crave the attention, even though at that point the threat is not identified with any would-be killer. I wouldn't totally rule out another anarchist, but I believe that we should explore other possibilities in the time that we have available to us."

Again, Rafferty spoke. "We certainly agree with that, Mr Holmes. But we're quite desperate, here. We don't want this to get out to the general public for fear of truly widespread panic. But we have a couple of days before the President arrives. What do you think we should do?"

"At the moment, I think you should do nothing," said Holmes. "Watson and I shall retire to our hotel to rest after our journey. I would suggest that we reconvene this evening at eight to start to formulate a plan. Please invite the chief of police."

"Wouldn't that be wasting six hours?" snapped Kenneally.

"Not for me," replied Holmes. "We have made some progress already this afternoon. I believe that we already know who the would-be assassin *isn't*. And that's important progress. We have two days to discover who he is! Come Watson; let's walk over to our hotel. I need to clear my head."

✗　✗　✗　✗

We left the Mayor's office with Rafferty in the lead. We proceeded down the stairs and exited City Hall onto the street, through the rear entry. We urged Rafferty to go ahead and make sure that there was no record of a Holmes or a Watson on the hotel register, and to pick up two keys for us.

"Let's walk around the block," said Holmes. "We need to give Rafferty a bit of time to make our stay anonymous."

I turned to Holmes as we walked. "Holmes, why are you so sure that our would-be assassin is not another anarchist? You seemed to have come to that conclusion rather quickly."

"My dear fellow," he replied. "You know me well enough to know that I never blurt out a conclusion without having thought about it. In this instance, I do feel quite certain. One can never rule out an event until we have determined that it's impossible, as I have mentioned to you before, so it's still possible that this could be a threat from an anarchist. But I don't think so. Beyond what I said upstairs about a threat in advance, rather than a credit-taking afterward, two other aspects of the warning note strike me as important. The first is the misspelling of the President's name. Someone who is intent on changing the world order by killing a president would probably have his name down pat. The second is the use of the word *execute*. That's an unusual word to use when one intends to say *murder*. To me the use of that term brings with it quite a different frame of reference. No, Watson, I think that we're looking for somebody who's closer to home."

"I tend to agree, Holmes, but it may take some work to convince the fellows upstairs."

"My thought exactly," he replied. "That's why I am going to keep the assassin discussion alive while you and I are exploring who else would want to kill President Roosevelt. I hope to convince the police chief to chase the assassin theory and to add a full layer of security over and above the Secret Service once the President arrives, and particularly at the event in the hotel ballroom. That certainly will not be a wasted use of police resources. But if in so doing we can keep him distracted with that business, it should give us the license to pursue all other avenues of inquiry. We will need all the freedom of movement that we can get, given that we have very few hours to find the would-be killer and stop him."

"How do we start, Holmes?"

"Let's begin by getting some rest. I suggest that we go to the hotel and settle in. We're to be back at City Hall at eight o'clock. Let's reconvene in our parlour over a room-service dinner at seven o'clock and lay out a strategy."

✗ ✗ ✗ ✗

When we arrived at the hotel, we found that Rafferty indeed had checked us in under assumed names and that our suite was ready for us. Holmes chose to retire to his bedroom to nap; I decided to explore the hotel.

I began by walking the corridor on our floor. I popped into the exit stairwell which only lead down, since we were on the top floor. I walked each floor, noting nothing unusual. I came off the stairwell at the second level, which housed the ballroom and several smaller meeting rooms. The Grand Ballroom was indeed a grand space: one large ballroom with an open balcony around its entire perimeter. The balcony interested me, so I walked up another interior stair to it. It consisted of numerous open areas, but also six private theatre-style compartments. I made a mental note to describe the balcony to Holmes. The compartments, which would probably not be in use for the Presidential dinner, would be an ideal hiding place for a shooter with a rifle. Any of the six compartments would command an unobstructed view of the entire ballroom.

I walked out the front door onto Main Street and strolled around the block on which the hotel was situated. I wanted to look at any other entrances and the loading dock, to see if anything struck me as unusual. Nothing did, so I went back into the hotel and took the elevator up to the sixth floor.

When I arrived at our floor, I encountered a room service waiter pushing a cart ahead of me. We arrived at room 625 simultaneously. I opened the door with my key and ushered him inside. Holmes was sitting in the parlour reading from the hotel information brochure.

"Ah, Jones, you've arrived just in time. I took the liberty of ordering dinner for both of us. I found roast mutton on the menu, with all the fixings."

"You've done well, Smith," I said with a bit of a chuckle. "Mrs Hudson would be quite pleased with your choice."

⚔   ⚔   ⚔   ⚔

We ate our meal, making small talk about the food and the differences between the roast lamb that our landlady on Baker Street routinely serves, and what the hotel put out. Truth be told, the American version proved to be quite good.

Holmes then began our strategy session.

"Watson, I think that we must make good use of our time tomorrow morning. I don't think that we'll accomplish much at City Hall tonight, although I'm interested in hearing what, if anything, the Police Chief has in mind as a response to the letter. As I said, I think that we must encourage him to stay on the anarchist theory, primarily to keep him out of our way over the next two days, but also because there is some chance—slim, in my opinion, but some—that his work might prove fruitful."

"I agree. That takes care of him. What do you see us doing in the morning to try to get out ahead of this?"

Holmes was quiet for a short time and then looked at me and said, "I think that we need to split up. I've arranged for an early meeting with the manager of the hotel. I want to review the registrations of everybody who's currently a guest in the hotel, and also of guests who will check in the next two days."

"What do you hope to find?"

"I have no idea. I admit that it's a single straw in a haystack, but someone or something may strike me as being of interest. I also plan to review the personnel files of every current employee in the hotel, and anybody who has left the employ of the hotel in the past six months. I'm hoping that something jumps out at me."

"Then I hope that you find something of interest. What should I be doing in the morning?"

"Watson, I'm leaving the difficult part for you. I'd like you to have Rafferty arrange a meeting with the editor of *The Springfield Republican*, which apparently is the newspaper of record here. I'd like you to review anything in the files about the period in 1898 and 1899 when Theodore Roosevelt was serving as Governor of New York State."

"I didn't know that he had been Governor," I offered. "I thought that he'd been elected Vice President and then succeeded McKinley after his assassination."

"I remember reading about him in our own *Times* when he became President. Actually, if I recall correctly, he was not elected Vice President but rather was appointed by the Congress when the sitting Vice President became ill and died in office. Prior to that, he had been briefly the Governor of New York, and a number of years earlier he had been the Police Commissioner of New York City."

"A remarkable ascension, from a head bobby to President of the United States. Only in this wild and woolly country could such an unlikely sequence of events occur."

"Well said, Watson, but don't let any thoughts that we might have about this upstart republic get in the way of what we must do in the next two days."

"Agreed, Holmes. What do you want me to look for?"

"If I knew the answer to that, we'd be well on our way to a solution. I'm hoping, since Springfield is very close to the New York state capital in Albany, that *The Republican* covers New York state news as well as national news. I'd like you to prevail upon the editor to walk you through his archives, looking for anything intriguing from late 1898 through 1899 that has to do with Roosevelt's term as Governor."

"What kinds of things would you expect me to find?"

"Anything that strikes your interest. Anything that might be controversial. Maybe something important. Maybe nothing. We're both grasping for straws, here. Let's see if one of us can find one to grab onto."

✗　✗　✗　✗

The meeting at City Hall proved uneventful. The group was assembled in the Mayor's Office with Rafferty. The one newcomer was a round, blustery fellow in a police uniform. He was introduced as Armand Ravida, Chief of the Springfield Police Department. He gave Holmes and me a perfunctory handshake and went back to what was obviously a conversation underway when we arrived.

"As I was saying, we need to canvas the Polish community in town. I believe that we have an anarchist in our midst, maybe more than one. And if we do, that's where we'll find them. Beginning tomorrow morning I'm going to have my street cops going door to door in our Little Poland. I'll be very surprised if we don't nip this supposed plot in the bud."

The Mayor turned to Holmes and said, "What do you think of that strategy, Mr Holmes?"

"I think it makes every bit of sense to begin the search there. The Chief obviously knows the neighborhoods and any hotbeds of political activity in the city. And he has the resources at his disposal to conduct a sweep."

"Won't that alert the entire city to the fear that we have an assassin on our hands?" posited Rafferty. "We're trying to avoid a wide spread panic, if we can."

"I think the Chief is an experienced hand at this sort of thing. I'm certain he'll handle it with the required discretion," said Holmes, with what I detected to be a slight bit of sarcasm.

Nobody else in the room seemed to have noticed Holmes's tone. The Chief's massive medal-strewn chest swelled at what he took to be a compliment from an equal in the business of fighting crime.

Holmes proceeded to describe, offering little detail, our plans for the next morning. The group reacted quietly, almost disappointedly, to his recital. It was almost as if they had expected the world's greatest detective to have the matter solved by lunch-time.

We made plans to meet the following evening at the same time to review that day's progress. The hope was expressed, somewhat pointedly by the Mayor, that we had some progress on which to report.

Holmes and I stood. We said our goodbyes and left the Mayor's office. When we reached the street, again by the back door, and began walking back to our hotel I said to Holmes, "What do you think of Chief Ravida?"

"I think that he's a clown," he said with a smile. "But at least he's out of our way. That was all that I'd hoped for from tonight's meeting. Tomorrow promises to be an interesting day."

✗　✗　✗　✗

When I awoke in the morning, after a fitful night's sleep, I came into the parlour expecting to find Holmes thinking about breakfast. Instead I found a note saying he would be back by early afternoon and he would meet me then. There was no indication of where he was going or what he was doing, but that was typical of Holmes.

I took my breakfast alone in the hotel dining room which was pleasant enough, although I vastly preferred our own English version. I went back to our suite to get my outer clothes and a notebook and headed off down Main Street to the headquarters of *The Springfield Republican*.

When I arrived, I found that Rafferty had done his work well. The editor, quite an engaging fellow called Charles Lowry, greeted me in the lobby and ushered me immediately up through the bustling newsroom and into his office.

"Dr Watson, it is a pleasure to meet you. Finn Rafferty told me that you needed to have a look at our archives for some information on President Roosevelt. What exactly do you want to review? We have excellent archives, at least for the past five years, thanks to this new invention called microfilm," said Lowry.

"I've heard of it, but never seen it. What I need to look at is anything about Roosevelt during the time that he was Governor of New York," I said.

"That should be relatively easy," offered Lowry. "Roosevelt was only Governor for a little more than one year. My recollection is that before being elected Governor he was the Police Commissioner of New York City for a number of years. Will you have any interest in those years?"

"I suppose that will depend on what we find in the gubernatorial year," I said, probably sounding more hopeful than I was feeling.

"Let's get at it then. I'll take you to the microfilm room and get you set up."

✗   ✗   ✗   ✗

Four hours later I thanked Lowry for his help and headed back to the hotel. In the hour that I spent looking at the years during which Roosevelt was Governor I found only a few items of news that barely met Holmes's instruction of things that struck my interest. For the balance of my time I examined his years as New York City Police Commissioner and found absolutely nothing of interest. It appeared that he was much respected in the city and seemed to have avoided controversy of any kind.

I let myself into our suite, not expecting that Holmes would be back from his morning's effort, presumably with the hotel manager.

To my surprise he was sitting at the dining table in the parlour with piles of folders spread out before him.

"Good afternoon, Watson," he said, looking up. "I hope that you had a more successful morning than I did."

"I'm not sure that I did. *The Republican* has a very modern archive system, which made it easy to review news stories, certainly as recent as the year 1899. That said, I didn't find much of anything. There were only one or two situations, but I'm afraid my efforts aren't going help us very much. What did you find out?"

"About the same: not much. I spent the morning with the general manager here, a proper German hotelier named Werner Schultz. I reviewed the guest list of the hotel from tonight through the weekend, including the night of the President's dinner. Many of the weekend guests are members of the Sierra Club, as one would expect. They certainly won't make our suspect list. As for the balance, it's hard to tell much from a list of names."

"Did you find any Polish names?" I asked, more in jest than in the belief that it would have meant anything.

"Not a one. I'm leaving the Polish witch hunt to our friend Ravida."

"What are all these folders?" I asked, pointing at the piles in front of Holmes.

"Employee personnel files. All current employees, and those who have left the hotel in the past three months."

"Anything of interest there?"

"It's hard to know. There are eighty current employees and twenty more who have left the hotel recently. It appears to be quite a stable group. Most of the employees have been here for a number of years. At this point it doesn't give us much to go on. Why don't you tell me what you've found?"

"Well, there is one interesting news story from March 1899. It has to do with the execution of a murderer that took place on Roosevelt's watch. This was apparently the only execution in the state of New York that year. *The Republican* reported that on March 20,

1899, a woman was put to death in the electric chair at New York's Sing Sing prison. She was the first woman in America to be killed using the chair that our American cousins refer to as 'Old Sparky.'"

"What else do we know about her?"

"Her name was Martha Place. She was convicted of bludgeoning her step-daughter to death in February 1898."

"This could be something that might make one hold a grudge," offered Holmes. "Maybe a grudge that would make one want to retaliate. Or even kill for revenge."

I flipped through the notes I'd taken at *The Republican*. "The news report says that she was born in New Jersey in 1849. Her birth name was Martha Garretson. She married a widower named William Place and moved with him to Brooklyn. The murder victim was Place's daughter from his earlier marriage."

"It would appear that Garretson and her step-daughter didn't get along very well," mused Holmes.

"So it would seem."

"Did it mention anything else about her?" he asked, his interest seeming to flag.

"Her husband testified against her at the trial and her brother—one Thomas Garretson—publicly protested her innocence. He claimed that she had been brain damaged in a carriage accident as a young woman and that her mental condition should have been taken into consideration at her trial, particularly at her sentencing. Apparently, he often staged a one-man protest in front of her prison, right up through the night of her execution."

"Anything more about the brother?" asked Holmes.

"It seems that he appealed to the Governor to commute the death sentence, which Roosevelt refused to do. On the night of the execution, Garretson was arrested for a disorderly protest outside the prison in Ossining."

"What became of him?"

"The press files indicate that he was released from the lockup the next morning and disappeared," I said, putting my notes away.

"An interesting tale, Watson, although I don't know how it helps us."

"I had certainly hoped for more, Holmes, but it would appear that Roosevelt's brief term as Governor was quite uneventful, as was his longer stint as Police Commissioner."

"My dear fellow, it was a shot in the dark at best. Probably a miss …. Although the name Thomas Garretson sounds familiar. Yet I don't know why it would. I can't recall ever having heard that surname before."

"Could he possibly be a guest in the hotel?" I asked. "That would put the name in the hotel's ledger."

Holmes suddenly seemed energized again. "I don't think so. But your question makes me think about something else," he said as he grabbed the pile of personnel files and started flipping through them.

He remained silent as he worked his way through the stack of folders, and then he stopped at one and studied it.

"Here's a fellow called Garrett Thomas," he said. "He's listed as being a room service waiter. Started his employment in January 1901. His file shows two former employers in Brooklyn. Can you tell from your notes how old this Martha Place was at the time of her execution?"

"The newspaper reported that she was fifty years old."

"About the same age as this Thomas fellow would have been at the time," he said, again referring to the file. "By any chance did the news report list a date of birth for the executed murderer?"

"I don't recall having seen it on the microfilm, but I must have, since I wrote a date into my notes. DOB: September 18, 1849."

"An interesting coincidence, Watson. The file on our man Thomas lists the same birth date."

"Holmes, are you suggesting …"

"I am. I believe that there is a strong possibility that the missing Thomas Garretson is the twin brother of Martha Place. He resurfaced a year ago with a new name, similar to his old name."

"To avoid the shame of being related to the only woman executed in the notorious electric chair, but without having to create an entirely new identity," I offered.

"Precisely, Watson. Good work this morning. Go back to your friend at *The Republican* and see if he has a photograph of Martha Place on file. I'm certain that there would have been one. With that in hand, I suggest we meet with Schultz, the manager here. The photograph can confirm any likeness to Garret Thomas, and then we can quickly schedule a meeting with Rafferty, the Mayor, and Ravida."

"I'm off, Holmes. As you're fond of saying, 'the game is afoot.'"

"Do hurry, Watson. We have no time to lose. Roosevelt is due in Springfield early tomorrow morning."

⚹ ⚹ ⚹ ⚹

Two hours later, Holmes and I, along with Werner Schultz, walked up the stairs in City Hall to the Mayor's office. Lowry at *The Republican* was able to produce a news photo of Martha Place from her trial. We showed the photo to Schultz and he confirmed what we'd suspected: the woman in the photo from the newspaper bore a striking resemblance to his employee Garrett Thomas. Schultz agreed to join us at the City Hall meeting, where we would decide our next steps.

We met Finbar Rafferty in front of the Mayor's office.

"Mr Holmes," said Rafferty. "I just heard from the Mayor that you've summoned a meeting with him and Ravida. I hope that means that you've made some progress, because I don't think that the Chief has done much other than stir up the Polish community."

"Watson and I have made some progress, which we shall share with the group. At the moment we have reason to believe that we've identified a person of interest, as they say at Scotland Yard."

"A person of strong interest," I chimed in.

"We'll see soon enough."

We knocked and entered. The Mayor and the Chief were already sitting at the Mayor's conference table.

"Come in, gentlemen, come in. We think that Chief Ravida is getting very close," said Kenneally.

Holmes and I looked at each other. "Excellent," said Holmes. "Watson and I can use all the help that we can get."

We listened without comment to Ravida's grandiose description of his department's sweep of the Polish neighborhoods in Springfield, including the fact that he had six men in custody.

The Mayor looked across the table at Holmes. "What do you think, Mr Holmes? Does this wrap it up?"

"It may well. Indeed, it may well. You and your men are to be commended. But do let me tell you what Watson and I have discovered."

Holmes proceeded to go through our meeting of the morning, step by step. When he got to the point at which he described our presumption that Garrett Thomas was in fact Thomas Garretson, the twin brother of the murderess, there was silence in the room.

To his credit, Werner Schultz broke the silence. "I've looked at the photograph of this woman. There is no doubt in my mind that the dead woman and my employee are twins."

Ravida was first to respond. "If that's the case I'll personally go to his house, wherever it is, and arrest him. I will drag him out in chains and keep him under lock and key until this event with Roosevelt is over."

"With respect, sir, I don't think that arresting him is the best idea," said Holmes. "We don't know for sure at this point that he has committed a crime. It would be very difficult to prove that he wrote the threatening letter."

"What do you suggest then, Mr Holmes?" said Kenneally. "We can't just sit on our hands."

"I assure you, Watson and I have no intention of sitting on our hands. I suggest that we set a trap for Garrett Thomas at the hotel, with the support of our friend Schultz, who has assured us of his full cooperation."

Holmes proceeded to tell the group exactly how to set the trap for the following morning. It would take place in the Presidential Suite, shortly after the President arrived at the hotel from Union Station.

The parties agreed. Only Ravida was muttering under his breath.

✗   ✗   ✗   ✗

The following morning, Holmes and I had an early breakfast in our suite and again went over the plan.

"Holmes, I like the plan. I do. I think that it's a brilliant deception. Assuming, of course, that Thomas is our man. What I don't fancy is that I'm to be the cheese in your mousetrap."

"My dear fellow, you'll be perfectly safe. I'll be in the coat closet and Ravida and two of his detectives will be in the powder room just off the Presidential parlour. As soon as Thomas begins to make a move, if he does, we'll spring the trap and subdue him."

"That gives me some comfort, but why does somebody need to impersonate President Roosevelt in the first place? Why can't he be at the table waiting for his lunch?"

"Several reasons. First, the Secret Service would never allow the President to be part of a plan to catch a criminal in the act, even if he were willing to play the role. But more importantly," continued my friend, "is the fact that you bear a striking resemblance to Roosevelt. You are roughly the same size and shape. You each have the same bushy mustache. I think that you're a perfect stand-in for the President. The more so, since Thomas will only see your back as he approaches the table."

"It's nice to know that I have attained perfection at something after a lengthy career."

Holmes chuckled. "Watson, you're among the most stalwart men I've known. You've saved my life at least twice over the years, and I would never put you at risk if I thought that the outcome for you would be dire."

"I certainly hope that the outcome is as benign as you are projecting it to be."

"The only person whose life is in danger is that of Garrett Thomas. And I'll make every effort to see that he's healthy enough to face justice."

"When do we go into action, Holmes?"

"As soon as Roosevelt arrives at the hotel, we'll take him into Schultz's office and brief him and his Secret Service people on the situation. Then you'll go up to the Presidential Suite, along with the Secret Service. Schultz has already ordered a light luncheon, as if from the Presidential party. Thomas is in the kitchen and Schultz has made arrangements for Thomas to deliver the meal."

Almost as an afterthought, Holmes mused, "The trap is set. The bait is in place. The supporting actors know their roles. As soon as you're upstairs impersonating Roosevelt, the curtain will rise."

✗ ✗ ✗ ✗

The meeting with Roosevelt went exactly as Holmes had predicted. The President was to remain in the safety of Schultz's office. I'd assume the role of the President and await my luncheon.

I was sitting at the large dining table with what appeared to be several small piles of work-related papers. My back was to the door. As a precaution, in the event the plan went completely awry, a small-caliber handgun had been concealed among the stacks of papers. Holmes was hidden in the closet immediately off the parlour, with the door slightly open to give him a line of sight to the table at which I was sitting. Ravida and one of his detectives were hidden in the powder room on the other side of the corridor. A Secret Service agent was in the bath off the bedroom, noisily running water to suggest that he was temporarily preoccupied, when all the while he was standing behind the half-open door with his pistol at the ready.

Soon there was a knock, followed by a voice announcing, "Room service, Mr President."

"Please come in. The door is open," I said, in my best American accent.

The door opened, and I turned slightly to glance at the waiter. He did indeed look like the photograph of Martha Place.

"Would you roll that over here like a good fellow?" I said, while turning my back to him and appearing to be going back to my paperwork.

"Absolutely, sir," said Thomas. "Welcome to the Massasoit Hotel. It is a pleasure to serve you."

"That's kind of you. Please leave the cart here by my table. I'll have my Secret Service agent find you with a gratuity later. He's indisposed at the moment."

"That won't be necessary, sir," he said. "I hope that you have a comfortable stay in Springfield."

"Indeed I shall," I said. "And thank you very much."

I heard him walking away. I tensed, waiting for the trap to spring. So far, Thomas hadn't done anything unexpected. Perhaps Holmes and I had been wrong from the beginning. I heard the door shut, and Thomas had obviously left the suite.

A few seconds passed, and I'd just begun to turn in my chair to commiserate with Holmes when I heard an angry voice.

"Executioner! Your own time has come," said the guttural voice.

I froze. My military training did not kick in. I slowly turned to face my attacker. Just then the closet door crashed open and Holmes burst into the room.

Holmes shouted, "Drop that gun!"

A crack, like wood against bone, echoed and a piece of Holmes's walking stick flew in the air, barely missing my head. A small black handgun skittered across the floor.

I turned to see Holmes wrestling on the floor with Thomas.

Then Ravida bellowed, charging out with his gun drawn. "Garrett Thomas, you're under arrest!" He was joined by the Secret Service agent racing from the bedroom who dove onto the pair on the floor. Without hesitating he slammed Thomas on the side of the head with the butt of his pistol. Thomas was unconscious.

Holmes got back to his feet, adjusted his clothing, and looked at his broken walking stick. He picked up the stub end from the floor and handed it to Ravida.

"Chief Ravida," said Holmes, "take this piece of my walking stick as a souvenir of your effort to keep your President safe. Thomas shouldn't cause you any more trouble. I'm happy to say that you can charge him with attempted murder, rather than murder."

"Mr Holmes, your modest assistance was quite valuable to our effort," said Ravida, with his self-congratulatory tone firmly in place.

Holmes looked at me, rolling his eyes slightly. "Chief, you can handle things from here. Come, Watson, we have to catch our train to Boston."

He waved rather than offering his hand. I did the same, and we turned and left Ravida to deal with the would-be assassin, who appeared to be regaining consciousness. We did indeed have a train to catch, although I think Holmes wanted to put some distance between himself and Ravida.

✗   ✗   ✗   ✗

We were sitting in the hotel lobby waiting for our carriage when Finn Rafferty joined us to say good-bye. Soon Mayor Kenneally burst through the revolving door into the lobby.

"Mr Holmes, Doctor! I'm so glad I caught you. The President wishes to thank you in person. Schultz called to tell me that he was on his way down to the lobby in hopes of finding you."

A soft chime rang, and the elevator door opened. Out came Roosevelt, followed by his Secret Service agents. We stood to greet the President. As he approached, I had to agree—to myself, of course—that we were quite similar in visage.

"Mr Holmes. Dr Watson. I'm deeply in your debt, as is my country."

"Mr President," said Holmes, offering his hand. "We're pleased to have been of assistance. It was as much luck as any special talent that we brought to the problem. It's pure coincidence that Watson and I happened to be coming through Springfield when the crisis arose. If there is a hero, it certainly must be young Rafferty here, who had the presence of mind to contact his brother in Minnesota, which set the chain of events in motion."

"Call it luck; call it coincidence, if you must," said Mr Roosevelt. "To me it was a case of brilliant sleuthing and intuitive analysis, following a very scant pattern of facts. The public shall never know how close this came to becoming a national disaster."

"That secret will be safe with us, Mr President," I said. "This episode will not find its way into one of my magazine chronicles. I can assure you of that."

"That gives me comfort, Doctor. Thank you."

Turning to Holmes, Roosevelt said, "I understand that you broke your walking stick over the skull of my assailant. I would like to replace it. Take mine as a keepsake." He handed Holmes a handsome ebony stick with an inlay of the Presidential Seal on the knob.

"Thank you, Mr President. I shall use this with pride. And I promise that I won't break it over anyone's head. Unless, of course, in a case of dire emergency."

Roosevelt chuckled, and offered his hand once again. "I must be on my way. I have to prepare my remarks for the Sierra Club meeting. Thank you both for your help. I shall never forget what you've done for me. And if you find yourself on our fair shores again, please send a message to me. It would be my pleasure to have you as my guests and give me an opportunity to catch up on the current state of crime detection, which, as you may know, was once my occupation in New York City."

With that, he turned and walked back toward the elevator with his Secret Service agent in tow.

✗　✗　✗　✗

Holmes and I were sitting on the first class deck of the RMS *Campania*, about an hour out of New York City on our way to Liverpool, after which we would train back home to London. The sun was high in a blue, cloudless sky. It was a beautiful day to be on the open water.

Holmes appeared to be sleeping, although I knew he wasn't. He was simply not in a mood for conversation. He was often like that after the conclusion of a case.

Ignoring his pretense, I said, "You know, Holmes, America is an interesting country. Still very much like what we see in the Wild West shows that come around from time to time. Seems quite a bit less civilized than our own glorious empire."

He opened an eye and responded: "You must remember, my dear fellow, that it's a very young country."

I let the thought sink in and then said, "I'd like to come back one day. To take Roosevelt up on his offer."

"Indeed. I expect Shadwell will have another assignment for us at some point. We'll be back."

We both fell silent, enjoying the view of the endless expanse of ocean.

After a spell of daydreaming, the vista reminded me of something I had read regarding our coming back to America.

"Holmes," I said, "I found a copy of a recent London *Times* in the hotel. It seems that the White Star Line has commissioned another liner to be even bigger and faster than the *Campania*. She's still quite a few years away from being christened, but we should make a point of following her progress."

"Maybe we'll book our next crossing on her and be part of breaking the speed record for a crossing. Have they given her a name yet?"

"They have. She's to be called *Titanic*. RMS *Titanic*."

✗

Terrence Guiney is a retired Boston hotel developer who writes crime fiction as a hobby. He is currently part of a group attempting to re-open the historic Hotel Massasoit in Springfield Mass, where this story is set and he is working on another history-based story of Holmes's exploits in America.

THE ADVENTURE OF THE PRIORY SCHOOL

by Sir Arthur Conan Doyle

We have had some dramatic entrances and exits upon our small stage at Baker Street, but I cannot recollect anything more sudden and startling than the first appearance of Dr Thorneycroft Huxtable, M.A., Ph.D., *etc*. His card, which seemed too small to carry the weight of his academic distinctions, preceded him by a few seconds, and then he entered himself—so large, so pompous, and so dignified that he was the very embodiment of self-possession and solidity. And yet his first action, when the door had closed behind him, was to stagger against the table, whence he slipped down upon the floor, and there was that majestic figure prostrate and insensible upon our bearskin hearthrug.

We had sprung to our feet, and for a few moments we stared in silent amazement at this ponderous piece of wreckage, which told of some sudden and fatal storm far out on the ocean of life. Then Holmes hurried with a cushion for his head, and I with brandy for his lips. The heavy, white face was seamed with lines of trouble, the hanging pouches under the closed eyes were leaden in colour, the loose mouth drooped dolorously at the corners, the rolling chins were unshaven. Collar and shirt bore the grime of a long journey, and the hair bristled unkempt from the well-shaped head. It was a sorely stricken man who lay before us.

"What is it, Watson?" asked Holmes.

"Absolute exhaustion—possibly mere hunger and fatigue," said I, with my finger on the thready pulse, where the stream of life trickled thin and small.

"Return ticket from Mackleton, in the north of England," said Holmes, drawing it from the watch-pocket. "It is not twelve o'clock yet. He has certainly been an early starter."

The puckered eyelids had begun to quiver, and now a pair of vacant grey eyes looked up at us. An instant later the man had scrambled on to his feet, his face crimson with shame.

"Forgive this weakness, Mr Holmes; I have been a little over-wrought. Thank you, if I might have a glass of milk and a biscuit I have no doubt that I should be better. I came personally, Mr Holmes, in order to insure that you would return with me. I feared that no telegram would convince you of the absolute urgency of the case."

"When you are quite restored—"

"I am quite well again. I cannot imagine how I came to be so weak. I wish you, Mr Holmes, to come to Mackleton with me by the next train."

My friend shook his head.

"My colleague, Dr Watson, could tell you that we are very busy at present. I am retained in this case of the Ferrers Documents, and the Abergavenny murder is coming up for trial. Only a very important issue could call me from London at present."

"Important!" Our visitor threw up his hands. "Have you heard nothing of the abduction of the only son of the Duke of Holdernesse?"

"What! the late Cabinet Minister?"

"Exactly. We had tried to keep it out of the papers, but there was some rumour in the *Globe* last night. I thought it might have reached your ears."

Holmes shot out his long, thin arm and picked out Volume "H" in his encyclopaedia of reference.

"'Holdernesse, 6th Duke, K.G., P.C.'—half the alphabet! 'Baron Beverley, Earl of Carston'—dear me, what a list! 'Lord Lieutenant of Hallamshire, since 1900. Married Edith, daughter of Sir Charles Appledore, 1888. Heir and only child, Lord Saltire. Owns about two hundred and fifty thousand acres. Minerals in Lancashire and Wales. Address: Carlton House Terrace; Holdernesse Hall, Hallamshire; Carston Castle, Bangor, Wales. Lord of the Admiralty, 1872; Chief Secretary of State for—' Well, well, this man is certainly one of the greatest subjects of the Crown!"

"The greatest and perhaps the wealthiest. I am aware, Mr Holmes, that you take a very high line in professional matters, and that you are prepared to work for the work's sake. I may tell you, however, that his Grace has already intimated that a check for five thousand pounds will be handed over to the person who can tell him where his son is, and another thousand to him who can name the man or men who have taken him."

"It is a princely offer," said Holmes. "Watson, I think that we shall accompany Dr Huxtable back to the north of England. And now, Dr Huxtable, when you have consumed that milk, you will kindly tell me what has happened, when it happened, how it happened, and, finally, what Dr Thorneycroft Huxtable, of the Priory School, near Mackleton, has to do with the matter, and why he comes three days after an event—the state of your chin gives the date—to ask for my humble services."

Our visitor had consumed his milk and biscuits. The light had come back to his eyes and the colour to his cheeks, as he set himself with great vigour and lucidity to explain the situation.

"I must inform you, gentlemen, that the Priory is a preparatory school, of which I am the founder and principal. *Huxtable's Sidelights on Horace* may possibly recall my name to your memories. The Priory is, without exception, the best and most select preparatory school in England. Lord Leverstoke, the Earl of Blackwater, Sir Cathcart Soames—they all have intrusted their sons to me. But I felt that my school had reached its zenith when, weeks ago, the Duke of Holdernesse sent Mr James Wilder, his secretary, with the intimation that young Lord Saltire, ten years old, his only son and heir, was about to be committed to my charge. Little did I think that this would be the prelude to the most crushing misfortune of my life.

"On May 1st the boy arrived, that being the beginning of the summer term. He was a charming youth, and he soon fell into our ways. I may tell you—I trust that I am not indiscreet, but half-confidences are absurd in such a case—that he was not entirely happy at home. It is an open secret that the Duke's married life had not been a peaceful one, and the matter had ended in a separation by mutual consent, the Duchess taking up her residence in the south of France. This had occurred very shortly before, and the boy's sympathies are known to have been strongly with his mother. He moped after her departure from Holdernesse Hall, and it was for this reason that the Duke desired to send him to my establishment.

In a fortnight the boy was quite at home with us and was apparently absolutely happy.

"He was last seen on the night of May 13th—that is, the night of last Monday. His room was on the second floor, and was approached through another larger room, in which two boys were sleeping. These boys saw and heard nothing, so that it is certain that young Saltire did not pass out that way. His window was open, and there is a stout ivy plant leading to the ground. We could trace no footmarks below, but it is sure that this is the only possible exit.

"His absence was discovered at seven o'clock on Tuesday morning. His bed had been slept in. He had dressed himself fully, before going off, in his usual school suit of black Eton jacket and dark grey trousers. There were no signs that anyone had entered the room, and it is quite certain that anything in the nature of cries or a struggle would have been heard, since Caunter, the elder boy in the inner room, is a very light sleeper.

"When Lord Saltire's disappearance was discovered, I at once called a roll of the whole establishment—boys, masters, and servants. It was then that we ascertained that Lord Saltire had not been alone in his flight. Heidegger, the German master, was missing. His room was on the second floor, at the farther end of the building, facing the same way as Lord Saltire's. His bed had also been slept in, but he had apparently gone away partly dressed, since his shirt and socks were lying on the floor. He had undoubtedly let himself down by the ivy, for we could see the marks of his feet where he had landed on the lawn. His bicycle was kept in a small shed beside this lawn, and it also was gone.

"He had been with me for two years, and came with the best references, but he was a silent, morose man, not very popular either with masters or boys. No trace could be found of the fugitives, and now, on Thursday morning, we are as ignorant as we were on Tuesday. Inquiry was, of course, made at once at Holdernesse Hall. It is only a few miles away, and we imagined that, in some sudden attack of homesickness, he had gone back to his father, but nothing had been heard of him. The Duke is greatly agitated—and, as to me, you have seen yourselves the state of nervous prostration to which the suspense and the responsibility have reduced me. Mr Holmes, if ever you put forward your full powers, I implore you to do so now, for never in your life could you have a case which is more worthy of them."

Sherlock Holmes had listened with the utmost intentness to the statement of the unhappy schoolmaster. His drawn brows and the deep furrow between them showed that he needed no exhortation to concentrate all his attention upon a problem which, apart from the tremendous interests involved, must appeal so directly to his love of the complex and the unusual. He now drew out his note-book and jotted down one or two memoranda.

"You have been very remiss in not coming to me sooner," said he severely. "You start me on my investigation with a very serious handicap. It is inconceivable, for example, that this ivy and this lawn would have yielded nothing to an expert observer."

"I am not to blame, Mr Holmes. His Grace was extremely desirous to avoid all public scandal. He was afraid of his family unhappiness being dragged before the world. He has a deep horror of anything of the kind."

"But there has been some official investigation?"

"Yes, sir, and it has proved most disappointing. An apparent clue was at once obtained, since a boy and a young man were reported to have been seen leaving a neighbouring station by an early train. Only last night we had news that the couple had been hunted down in Liverpool, and they prove to have no connection whatever with the matter in hand. Then it was that in my despair and disappointment, after a sleepless night, I came straight to you by the early train."

"I suppose the local investigation was relaxed while this false clue was being followed up?"

"It was entirely dropped."

"So that three days have been wasted. The affair has been most deplorably handled."

"I feel it and admit it."

"And yet the problem should be capable of ultimate solution. I shall be very happy to look into it. Have you been able to trace any connection between the missing boy and this German master?"

"None at all."

"Was he in the master's class?"

"No; he never exchanged a word with him, so far as I know."

"That is certainly very singular. Had the boy a bicycle?"

"No."

"Was any other bicycle missing?"

"No."

"Is that certain?"

"Quite."

"Well, now, you do not mean to seriously suggest that this German rode off upon a bicycle in the dead of the night bearing the boy in his arms?"

"Certainly not."

"Then what is the theory in your mind?"

"The bicycle may have been a blind. It may have been hidden somewhere, and the pair gone off on foot."

"Quite so, but it seems rather an absurd blind, does it not? Were there other bicycles in this shed?"

"Several."

"Would he not have hidden a *couple*, had he desired to give the idea that they had gone off upon them?"

"I suppose he would."

"Of course he would. The blind theory won't do. But the incident is an admirable starting-point for an investigation. After all, a bicycle is not an easy thing to conceal or to destroy. One other question. Did anyone call to see the boy on the day before he disappeared?"

"No."

"Did he get any letters?"

"Yes; one letter."

"From whom?"

"From his father."

"Do you open the boys' letters?"

"No."

"How do you know it was from the father?"

"The coat of arms was on the envelope, and it was addressed in the Duke's peculiar stiff hand. Besides, the Duke remembers having written."

"When had he a letter before that?"

"Not for several days."

"Had he ever one from France?"

"No; never."

"You see the point of my questions, of course. Either the boy was carried off by force or he went of his own free will. In the latter case, you would expect that some prompting from outside would be needed to make so young a lad do such a thing. If he has had no visitors, that prompting must have come in letters. Hence I try to find out who were his correspondents."

"I fear I cannot help you much. His only correspondent, so far as I know, was his own father."

"Who wrote to him on the very day of his disappearance. Were the relations between father and son very friendly?"

"His Grace is never very friendly with anyone. He is completely immersed in large public questions, and is rather inaccessible to all ordinary emotions. But he was always kind to the boy in his own way."

"But the sympathies of the latter were with the mother?"

"Yes."

"Did he say so?"

"No."

"The Duke, then?"

"Good heavens, no!"

"Then how could you know?"

"I have had some confidential talks with Mr James Wilder, his Grace's secretary. It was he who gave me the information about Lord Saltire's feelings."

"I see. By the way, that last letter of the Duke's—was it found in the boy's room after he was gone?"

"No; he had taken it with him. I think, Mr Holmes, it is time that we were leaving for Euston."

"I will order a four-wheeler. In a quarter of an hour we shall be at your service. If you are telegraphing home, Mr Huxtable, it would be well to allow the people in your neighbourhood to imagine that the inquiry is still going on in Liverpool, or wherever else that red herring led your pack. In the meantime, I will do a little quiet work at your own doors, and perhaps the scent is not so cold but that two old hounds like Watson and myself may get a sniff of it."

✗ ✗ ✗ ✗

That evening found us in the cold, bracing atmosphere of the Peak country, in which Dr Huxtable's famous school is situated. It was already dark when we reached it. A card was lying on the hall table, and the butler whispered something to his master, who turned to us with agitation in every heavy feature.

"The Duke is here," said he. "The Duke and Mr Wilder are in the study. Come, gentlemen, and I will introduce you."

I was, of course, familiar with the pictures of the famous statesman, but the man himself was very different from his representation. He was a tall and stately person, scrupulously dressed, with a drawn, thin face, and a nose which was grotesquely curved and long. His complexion was of a dead pallor, which was more startling by contrast with a long, dwindling beard of vivid red, which flowed down over his white waistcoat with his watch-chain gleaming through its fringe. Such was the stately presence who looked stonily at us from the centre of Dr Huxtable's hearthrug. Beside him stood a very young man, whom I understood to be Wilder, the private secretary. He was small, nervous, alert, with intelligent light-blue eyes and mobile features. It was he who at once, in an incisive and positive tone, opened the conversation.

"I called this morning, Dr Huxtable, too late to prevent you from starting for London. I learned that your object was to invite Mr Sherlock Holmes to undertake the conduct of this case. His Grace is surprised, Dr Huxtable, that you should have taken such a step without consulting him."

"When I learned that the police had failed—"

"His Grace is by no means convinced that the police have failed."

"But surely, Mr Wilder—"

"You are well aware, Dr Huxtable, that his Grace is particularly anxious to avoid all public scandal. He prefers to take as few people as possible into his confidence."

"The matter can be easily remedied," said the browbeaten doctor; "Mr Sherlock Holmes can return to London by the morning train."

"Hardly that, Doctor, hardly that," said Holmes, in his blandest voice. "This northern air is invigorating and pleasant, so I propose to spend a few days upon your moors, and to occupy my mind as best I may. Whether I have the shelter of your roof or of the village inn is, of course, for you to decide."

I could see that the unfortunate doctor was in the last stage of indecision, from which he was rescued by the deep, sonorous voice of the red-bearded Duke, which boomed out like a dinner-gong.

"I agree with Mr Wilder, Dr Huxtable, that you would have done wisely to consult me. But since Mr Holmes has already been taken into your confidence, it would indeed be absurd that we should not avail ourselves of his services. Far from going to the inn, Mr Holmes, I should be pleased if you would come and stay with me at Holdernesse Hall."

"I thank your Grace. For the purposes of my investigation, I think that it would be wiser for me to remain at the scene of the mystery."

"Just as you like, Mr Holmes. Any information which Mr Wilder or I can give you is, of course, at your disposal."

"It will probably be necessary for me to see you at the Hall," said Holmes. "I would only ask you now, sir, whether you have formed any explanation in your own mind as to the mysterious disappearance of your son?"

"No, sir, I have not."

"Excuse me if I allude to that which is painful to you, but I have no alternative. Do you think that the Duchess had anything to do with the matter?"

The great minister showed perceptible hesitation.

"I do not think so," he said, at last.

"The other most obvious explanation is that the child has been kidnapped for the purpose of levying ransom. You have not had any demand of the sort?"

"No, sir."

"One more question, your Grace. I understand that you wrote to your son upon the day when this incident occurred."

"No, I wrote upon the day before."

"Exactly. But he received it on that day?"

"Yes."

"Was there anything in your letter which might have unbalanced him or induced him to take such a step?"

"No, sir, certainly not."

"Did you post that letter yourself?"

The nobleman's reply was interrupted by his secretary, who broke in with some heat.

"His Grace is not in the habit of posting letters himself," said he. "This letter was laid with others upon the study table, and I myself put them in the post-bag."

"You are sure this one was among them?"

"Yes, I observed it."

"How many letters did your Grace write that day?"

"Twenty or thirty. I have a large correspondence. But surely this—is somewhat irrelevant?"

"Not entirely," said Holmes.

"For my own part," the Duke continued, "I have advised the police to turn their attention to the South of France. I have already said that I do not believe that the Duchess would encourage so monstrous an action, but the lad had the most wrong-headed opinions, and it is possible that he may have fled to her, aided and abetted by this German. I think, Dr Huxtable, that we will now return to the Hall."

I could see that there were other questions which Holmes would have wished to put but the nobleman's abrupt manner showed that the interview was at an end. It was evident that to his intensely aristocratic nature this discussion of his intimate family affairs with a stranger was most abhorrent, and that he feared lest every fresh question would throw a fiercer light into the discreetly shadowed corners of his ducal history.

When the nobleman and his secretary had left, my friend flung himself at once with characteristic eagerness into the investigation.

The boy's chamber was carefully examined, and yielded nothing save the absolute conviction that it was only through the window that he could have escaped. The German master's room and effects gave no further clue. In his case a trailer of ivy had given way under his weight, and we saw by the light of a lantern the mark on the lawn where his heels had come down. That one dint in the short, green grass was the only material witness left of this inexplicable nocturnal flight.

Sherlock Holmes left the house alone, and only returned after eleven. He had obtained a large ordnance map of the neighbourhood, and this he brought into my room, where he laid it out on the bed, and, having balanced the lamp in the middle of it, he began to smoke over it, and occasionally to point out objects of interest with the reeking amber of his pipe.

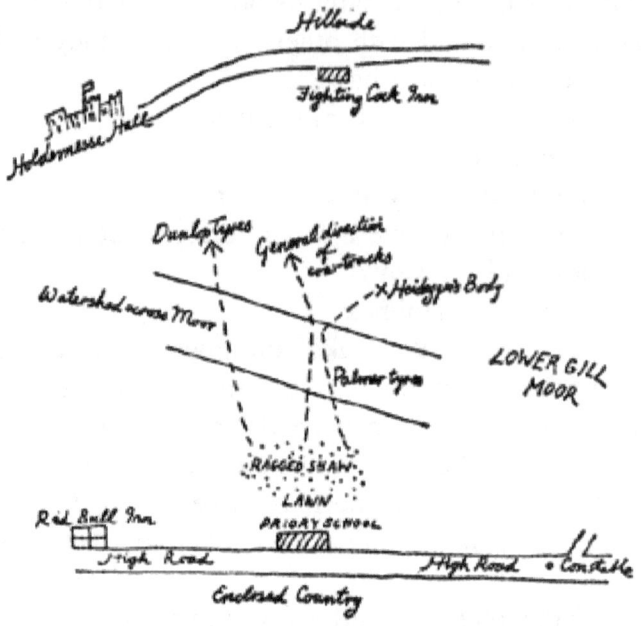

HOLMES'S MAP OF THE NEIGHBOURHOOD OF THE SCHOOL.

"This case grows upon me, Watson," said he. "There are decidedly some points of interest in connection with it. In this early stage, I want you to realize those geographical features which may have a good deal to do with our investigation.

"Look at this map. This dark square is the Priory School. I'll put a pin in it. Now, this line is the main road. You see that it runs east and west past the school, and you see also that there is no side road for a mile either way. If these two folk passed away by road, it was *this* road."

"Exactly."

"By a singular and happy chance, we are able to some extent to check what passed along this road during the night in question. At this point, where my pipe is now resting, a county constable was on duty from twelve to six. It is, as you perceive, the first cross-road on the east side. This man declares that he was not absent from his post for an instant, and he is positive that neither boy nor man could have gone that way unseen. I have spoken with this policeman to-night, and he appears to me to be a perfectly reliable person. That blocks this end. We have now to deal with the other. There is an inn here, the 'Red Bull', the landlady of which was ill. She had sent to Mackleton for a doctor, but he did not arrive until morning, being absent at another case. The people at the inn were alert all night, awaiting his coming, and one or other of them seems to have continually had an eye upon the road. They declare that no one passed. If their evidence is good, then we are fortunate enough to be able to block the west, and also to be able to say that the fugitives did *not* use the road at all."

"But the bicycle?" I objected.

"Quite so. We will come to the bicycle presently. To continue our reasoning: if these people did not go by the road, they must have traversed the country to the north of the house or to the south of the house. That is certain. Let us weigh the one against the other. On the south of the house is, as you perceive, a large district of arable land, cut up into small fields, with stone walls between them. There, I admit that a bicycle is impossible. We can dismiss the idea. We turn to the country on the north. Here there lies a grove of trees, marked as the 'Ragged Shaw,' and on the farther side stretches a great rolling moor, Lower Gill Moor, extending for ten miles and sloping gradually upward. Here, at one side of this wilderness, is Holdernesse Hall, ten miles by road, but only six across the moor. It is a peculiarly desolate plain. A few moor farmers have small holdings, where they rear sheep and cattle. Except these, the plover and the curlew are the only inhabitants until you come to the Chesterfield high road. There is a church there, you see, a few cottages, and an inn. Beyond that the hills become precipitous. Surely it is here to the north that our quest must lie."

"But the bicycle?" I persisted.

"Well, well!" said Holmes impatiently. "A good cyclist does not need a high road. The moor is intersected with paths, and the moon was at the full. Halloa! what is this?"

There was an agitated knock at the door, and an instant afterwards Dr Huxtable was in the room. In his hand he held a blue cricket-cap, with a white chevron on the peak.

"At last we have a clue!" he cried. "Thank heaven! at last we are on the dear boy's track! It is his cap."

"Where was it found?"

"In the van of the gipsies who camped on the moor. They left on Tuesday. To-day the police traced them down and examined their caravan. This was found."

"How do they account for it?"

"They shuffled and lied—said that they found it on the moor on Tuesday morning. They know where he is, the rascals! Thank goodness, they are all safe under lock and key. Either the fear of the law or the Duke's purse will certainly get out of them all that they know."

"So far, so good," said Holmes, when the doctor had at last left the room. "It at least bears out the theory that it is on the side of the Lower Gill Moor that we must hope for results. The police have really done nothing locally, save the arrest of these gipsies. Look here, Watson! There is a watercourse across the moor. You see it marked here in the map. In some parts it widens into a morass. This is particularly so in the region between Holdernesse Hall and the school. It is vain to look elsewhere for tracks in this dry weather; but at *that* point there is certainly a chance of some record being left. I will call you early to-morrow morning, and you and I will try if we can throw some little light upon the mystery."

The day was just breaking when I woke to find the long, thin form of Holmes by my bedside. He was fully dressed, and had apparently already been out.

"I have done the lawn and the bicycle shed," said he. "I have also had a ramble through the Ragged Shaw. Now, Watson, there is cocoa ready in the next room. I must beg you to hurry, for we have a great day before us."

His eyes shone, and his cheek was flushed with the exhilaration of the master workman who sees his work lie ready before him. A very different Holmes, this active, alert man, from the introspective and pallid dreamer of Baker Street. I felt, as I looked upon that supple figure, alive with nervous energy, that it was indeed a strenuous day that awaited us.

And yet it opened in the blackest disappointment. With high hopes we struck across the peaty, russet moor, intersected with a thousand sheep paths, until we came to the broad, light-green belt which marked the morass between us and Holdernesse. Certainly, if the lad had gone homeward, he must have passed this, and he could not pass it without leaving his traces. But no sign of him or the German could be seen. With a darkening face my friend strode along the margin, eagerly observant of every muddy stain upon the mossy surface. Sheep-marks there were in profusion, and at one place, some miles down, cows had left their tracks. Nothing more.

"Check number one," said Holmes, looking gloomily over the rolling expanse of the moor. "There is another morass down yonder, and a narrow neck between. Halloa! halloa! halloa! what have we here?"

We had come on a small black ribbon of pathway. In the middle of it, clearly marked on the sodden soil was the track of a bicycle.

"Hurrah!" I cried. "We have it."

But Holmes was shaking his head, and his face was puzzled and expectant rather than joyous.

"A bicycle, certainly, but not *the* bicycle," said he. "I am familiar with forty-two different impressions left by tyres. This, as you perceive, is a Dunlop, with a patch upon the outer cover. Heidegger's tires were Palmer's, leaving longitudinal stripes. Aveling, the mathematical master, was sure upon the point. Therefore, it is not Heidegger's track."

"The boy's, then?"

"Possibly, if we could prove a bicycle to have been in his possession. But this we have utterly failed to do. This track, as you perceive, was made by a rider who was going from the direction of the school."

"Or towards it?"

"No, no, my dear Watson. The more deeply sunk impression is, of course, the hind wheel, upon which the weight rests. You perceive several places where it has passed across and obliterated the more shallow mark of the front one. It was undoubtedly heading away from the school. It may or may not be connected with our inquiry, but we will follow it backwards before we go any farther."

We did so, and at the end of a few hundred yards lost the tracks as we emerged from the boggy portion of the moor. Following the path backwards, we picked out another spot, where a spring trickled across it. Here, once again, was the mark of the bicycle, though nearly obliterated by the hoofs of cows. After that there was no sign, but the path ran right on into Ragged Shaw, the wood which backed on to the school. From this wood the cycle must have emerged. Holmes sat down on a boulder and rested his chin in his hands. I had smoked two cigarettes before he moved.

"Well, well," said he, at last. "It is, of course, possible that a cunning man might change the tyres of his bicycle in order to leave unfamiliar tracks. A criminal who was capable of such a thought is a man whom I should be proud to do business with. We will leave this question undecided and hark back to our morass again, for we have left a good deal unexplored."

We continued our systematic survey of the edge of the sodden portion of the moor, and soon our perseverance was gloriously rewarded. Right across the lower part of the bog lay a miry path. Holmes gave a cry of delight as he approached it. An impression like a fine bundle of telegraph wires ran down the centre of it. It was the Palmer tyre.

"Here is Herr Heidegger, sure enough!" cried Holmes, exultantly. "My reasoning seems to have been pretty sound, Watson."

"I congratulate you."

"But we have a long way still to go. Kindly walk clear of the path. Now let us follow the trail. I fear that it will not lead very far."

We found, however, as we advanced, that this portion of the moor is intersected with soft patches, and, though we frequently lost sight of the track, we always succeeded in picking it up once more.

"Do you observe," said Holmes, "that the rider is now undoubtedly forcing the pace? There can be no doubt of it. Look at this impression, where you get both tyres clear. The one is as deep as the other. That can only mean that the rider is throwing his weight on to the handle-bar, as a man does when he is sprinting. By Jove! he has had a fall."

There was a broad, irregular smudge covering some yards of the track. Then there were a few footmarks, and the tyres reappeared once more.

"A side-slip," I suggested.

Holmes held up a crumpled branch of flowering gorse. To my horror I perceived that the yellow blossoms were all dabbled with crimson. On the path, too, and among the heather were dark stains of clotted blood.

"Bad!" said Holmes. "Bad! Stand clear, Watson! Not an unnecessary footstep! What do I read here? He fell wounded—he stood up—he remounted—he proceeded. But there is no other track. Cattle on this side path. He was surely not gored by a bull? Impossible! But I see no traces of anyone else. We must push on, Watson. Surely, with stains as well as the track to guide us, he cannot escape us now."

Our search was not a very long one. The tracks of the tyre began to curve fantastically upon the wet and shining path. Suddenly, as I looked ahead, the gleam of metal caught my eye from amid the thick gorse-bushes. Out of them we dragged a bicycle, Palmer-tyred, one pedal bent, and the whole front of it horribly smeared and slobbered with blood. On the other side of the bushes, a shoe was projecting. We ran round, and there lay the unfortunate rider. He was a tall man, full-bearded, with spectacles, one glass of which had been knocked out. The cause of his death was a frightful blow upon the head, which had crushed in part of his skull. That he could have gone on after receiving such an injury said much for the vitality and courage of the man. He wore shoes, but no socks, and his open coat disclosed a nightshirt beneath it. It was undoubtedly the German master.

Holmes turned the body over reverently, and examined it with great attention. He then sat in deep thought for a time, and I could see by his ruffled brow that this grim discovery had not, in his opinion, advanced us much in our inquiry.

"It is a little difficult to know what to do, Watson," said he, at last. "My own inclinations are to push this inquiry on, for we have already lost so much time that we cannot afford to waste another hour. On the other hand, we are bound to inform the police of the discovery, and to see that this poor fellow's body is looked after."

"I could take a note back."

"But I need your company and assistance. Wait a bit! There is a fellow cutting peat up yonder. Bring him over here, and he will guide the police."

I brought the peasant across, and Holmes despatched the frightened man with a note to Dr Huxtable.

"Now, Watson," said he, "we have picked up two clues this morning. One is the bicycle with the Palmer tyre, and we see what that has led to. The other is the bicycle with the patched Dunlop.

Before we start to investigate that, let us try to realize what we *do* know, so as to make the most of it, and to separate the essential from the accidental.

"First of all, I wish to impress upon you that the boy certainly left of his own free-will. He got down from his window and he went off, either alone or with someone. That is sure."

I assented.

"Well, now, let us turn to this unfortunate German master. The boy was fully dressed when he fled. Therefore, he foresaw what he would do. But the German went without his socks. He certainly acted on very short notice."

"Undoubtedly."

"Why did he go? Because, from his bedroom window, he saw the flight of the boy, because he wished to overtake him and bring him back. He seized his bicycle, pursued the lad, and in pursuing him met his death."

"So it would seem."

"Now I come to the critical part of my argument. The natural action of a man in pursuing a little boy would be to run after him. He would know that he could overtake him. But the German does not do so. He turns to his bicycle. I am told that he was an excellent cyclist. He would not do this if he did not see that the boy had some swift means of escape."

"The other bicycle."

"Let us continue our reconstruction. He meets his death five miles from the school—not by a bullet, mark you, which even a lad might conceivably discharge, but by a savage blow dealt by a vigorous arm. The lad, then, *had* a companion in his flight. And the flight was a swift one, since it took five miles before an expert cyclist could overtake them. Yet we survey the ground round the scene of the tragedy. What do we find? A few cattle-tracks, nothing more. I took a wide sweep round, and there is no path within fifty yards. Another cyclist could have had nothing to do with the actual murder, nor were there any human foot-marks."

"Holmes," I cried, "this is impossible."

"Admirable!" he said. "A most illuminating remark. It *is* impossible as I state it, and therefore I must in some respect have stated it wrong. Yet you saw for yourself. Can you suggest any fallacy?"

"He could not have fractured his skull in a fall?"

"In a morass, Watson?"

"I am at my wit's end."

"Tut, tut, we have solved some worse problems. At least we have plenty of material, if we can only use it. Come, then, and, having exhausted the Palmer, let us see what the Dunlop with the patched cover has to offer us."

We picked up the track and followed it onward for some distance; but soon the moor rose into a long, heather-tufted curve, and we left the watercourse behind us. No further help from tracks could be hoped for. At the spot where we saw the last of the Dunlop tyre it might equally have led to Holdernesse Hall, the stately towers of which rose some miles to our left, or to a low, grey village which lay in front of us and marked the position of the Chesterfield high road.

As we approached the forbidding and squalid inn, with the sign of a game-cock above the door, Holmes gave a sudden groan, and clutched me by the shoulder to save himself from falling. He had had one of those violent strains of the ankle which leave a man helpless. With difficulty he limped up to the door, where a squat, dark, elderly man was smoking a black clay pipe.

"How are you, Mr Reuben Hayes?" said Holmes.

"Who are you, and how do you get my name so pat?" the countryman answered, with a suspicious flash of a pair of cunning eyes.

"Well, it's printed on the board above your head. It's easy to see a man who is master of his own house. I suppose you haven't such a thing as a carriage in your stables?"

"No, I have not."

"I can hardly put my foot to the ground."

"Don't put it to the ground."

"But I can't walk."

"Well, then, hop."

Mr Reuben Hayes's manner was far from gracious, but Holmes took it with admirable good-humour.

"Look here, my man," said he. "This is really rather an awkward fix for me. I don't mind how I get on."

"Neither do I," said the morose landlord.

"The matter is very important. I would offer you a sovereign for the use of a bicycle."

The landlord pricked up his ears.

"Where do you want to go?"

"To Holdernesse Hall."

"Pals of the Dook, I suppose?" said the landlord, surveying our mud-stained garments with ironical eyes.

Holmes laughed good-naturedly.

"He'll be glad to see us, anyhow."

"Why?"

"Because we bring him news of his lost son."

The landlord gave a very visible start.

"What, you're on his track?"

"He has been heard of in Liverpool. They expect to get him every hour."

Again a swift change passed over the heavy, unshaven face. His manner was suddenly genial.

"I've less reason to wish the Dook well than most men," said he, "for I was head coachman once, and cruel bad he treated me. It was him that sacked me without a character on the word of a lying corn-chandler. But I'm glad to hear that the young lord was heard of in Liverpool, and I'll help you to take the news to the Hall."

"Thank you," said Holmes. "We'll have some food first. Then you can bring round the bicycle."

"I haven't got a bicycle."

Holmes held up a sovereign.

"I tell you, man, that I haven't got one. I'll let you have two horses as far as the Hall."

"Well, well," said Holmes, "we'll talk about it when we've had something to eat."

When we were left alone in the stone-flagged kitchen, it was astonishing how rapidly that sprained ankle recovered. It was nearly nightfall, and we had eaten nothing since early morning, so that we spent some time over our meal. Holmes was lost in thought, and once or twice he walked over to the window and stared earnestly out. It opened on to a squalid courtyard. In the far corner was a smithy, where a grimy lad was at work. On the other side were the stables. Holmes had sat down again after one of these excursions, when he suddenly sprang out of his chair with a loud exclamation.

"By heaven, Watson, I believe that I've got it!" he cried. "Yes, yes, it must be so. Watson, do you remember seeing any cow-tracks to-day?"

"Yes, several."

"Where?"

"Well, everywhere. They were at the morass, and again on the path, and again near where poor Heidegger met his death."

"Exactly. Well, now, Watson, how many cows did you see on the moor?"

"I don't remember seeing any."

"Strange, Watson, that we should see tracks all along our line, but never a cow on the whole moor; very strange, Watson, eh?"

"Yes, it is strange."

"Now, Watson, make an effort, throw your mind back. Can you see those tracks upon the path?"

"Yes, I can."

"Can you recall that the tracks were sometimes like that, Watson,"—he arranged a number of bread-crumbs in this fashion— : : : : :—"and sometimes like this"—: . : . : . : .—"and occasionally like this"—· . · . · . "Can you remember that?"

"No, I cannot."

"But I can. I could swear to it. However, we will go back at our leisure and verify it. What a blind beetle I have been not to draw my conclusion."

"And what is your conclusion?"

"Only that it is a remarkable cow which walks, canters, and gallops. By George, Watson, it was no brain of a country publican that thought out such a blind as that. The coast seems to be clear, save for that lad in the smithy. Let us slip out and see what we can see."

There were two rough-haired, unkempt horses in the tumble-down stable. Holmes raised the hind leg of one of them and laughed aloud.

"Old shoes, but newly shod—old shoes, but new nails. This case deserves to be a classic. Let us go across to the smithy."

The lad continued his work without regarding us. I saw Holmes's eye darting to right and left among the litter of iron and wood which was scattered about the floor. Suddenly, however, we heard a step behind us, and there was the landlord, his heavy eyebrows drawn over his savage eyes, his swarthy features convulsed with passion. He held a short, metal-headed stick in his hand, and he advanced in so menacing a fashion that I was right glad to feel the revolver in my pocket.

"You infernal spies!" the man cried. "What are you doing there?"

"Why, Mr Reuben Hayes," said Holmes, coolly, "one might think that you were afraid of our finding something out."

The man mastered himself with a violent effort, and his grim mouth loosened into a false laugh, which was more menacing than his frown.

"You're welcome to all you can find out in my smithy," said he. "But look here, mister, I don't care for folk poking about my place without my leave, so the sooner you pay your score and get out of this the better I shall be pleased."

"All right, Mr Hayes—no harm meant," said Holmes. "We have been having a look at your horses, but I think I'll walk, after all. It's not far, I believe."

"Not more than two miles to the Hall gates. That's the road to the left." He watched us with sullen eyes until we had left his premises.

We did not go very far along the road, for Holmes stopped the instant that the curve hid us from the landlord's view.

"We were warm, as the children say, at that inn," said he. "I seem to grow colder every step that I take away from it. No, no, I can't possibly leave it."

"I am convinced," said I, "that this Reuben Hayes knows all about it. A more self-evident villain I never saw."

"Oh! he impressed you in that way, did he? There are the horses, there is the smithy. Yes, it is an interesting place, this 'Fighting Cock'. I think we shall have another look at it in an unobtrusive way."

A long, sloping hillside, dotted with grey limestone boulders, stretched behind us. We had turned off the road, and were making our way up the hill, when, looking in the direction of Holdernesse Hall, I saw a cyclist coming swiftly along.

"Get down, Watson!" cried Holmes, with a heavy hand upon my shoulder. We had hardly sunk from view when the man flew past us on the road. Amid a rolling cloud of dust, I caught a glimpse of a pale, agitated face—a face with horror in every lineament, the mouth open, the eyes staring wildly in front. It was like some strange caricature of the dapper James Wilder whom we had seen the night before.

"The Duke's secretary!" cried Holmes. "Come, Watson, let us see what he does."

We scrambled from rock to rock, until in a few moments we had made our way to a point from which we could see the front door of the inn. Wilder's bicycle was leaning against the wall beside it. No one was moving about the house, nor could we catch a glimpse of any faces at the windows. Slowly the twilight crept down as the sun sank behind the high towers of Holdernesse Hall. Then, in the gloom, we saw the two side-lamps of a trap light up in the stable-yard of the inn, and shortly afterwards heard the rattle of hoofs, as it wheeled out into the road and tore off at a furious pace in the direction of Chesterfield.

"What do you make of that, Watson?" Holmes whispered.

"It looks like a flight."

"A single man in a dog-cart, so far as I could see. Well, it certainly was not Mr James Wilder, for there he is at the door."

A red square of light had sprung out of the darkness. In the middle of it was the black figure of the secretary, his head advanced, peering out into the night. It was evident that he was expecting someone. Then at last there were steps in the road, a second figure was visible for an instant against the light, the door shut, and all was black once more. Five minutes later a lamp was lit in a room upon the first floor.

"It seems to be a curious class of custom that is done by the 'Fighting Cock'," said Holmes.

"The bar is on the other side."

"Quite so. These are what one may call the private guests. Now, what in the world is Mr James Wilder doing in that den at this hour of night, and who is the companion who comes to meet him there? Come, Watson, we must really take a risk and try to investigate this a little more closely."

Together we stole down to the road and crept across to the door of the inn. The bicycle still leaned against the wall. Holmes struck a match and held it to the back wheel, and I heard him chuckle as the light fell upon a patched Dunlop tyre. Up above us was the lighted window.

"I must have a peep through that, Watson. If you bend your back and support yourself upon the wall, I think that I can manage."

An instant later, his feet were on my shoulders, but he was hardly up before he was down again.

"Come, my friend," said he, "our day's work has been quite long enough. I think that we have gathered all that we can. It's a long walk to the school, and the sooner we get started the better."

He hardly opened his lips during that weary trudge across the moor, nor would he enter the school when he reached it, but went on to Mackleton Station, whence he could send some telegrams. Late at night I heard him consoling Dr Huxtable, prostrated by the tragedy of his master's death, and later still he entered my room as alert and vigorous as he had been when he started in the morning. "All goes well, my friend," said he. "I promise that before to-morrow evening we shall have reached the solution of the mystery."

At eleven o'clock next morning my friend and I were walking up the famous yew avenue of Holdernesse Hall. We were ushered through the magnificent Elizabethan doorway and into his Grace's study. There we found Mr James Wilder, demure and courtly, but with some trace of that wild terror of the night before still lurking in his furtive eyes and in his twitching features.

"You have come to see his Grace? I am sorry; but the fact is that the Duke is far from well. He has been very much upset by the tragic news. We received a telegram from Dr Huxtable yesterday afternoon, which told us of your discovery."

"I must see the Duke, Mr Wilder."

"But he is in his room."

"Then I must go to his room."

"I believe he is in his bed."

"I will see him there."

Holmes's cold and inexorable manner showed the secretary that it was useless to argue with him.

"Very good, Mr Holmes, I will tell him that you are here."

After half an hour's delay, the great nobleman appeared. His face was more cadaverous than ever, his shoulders had rounded, and he seemed to me to be an altogether older man than he had been the morning before. He greeted us with a stately courtesy and seated himself at his desk, his red beard streaming down on the table.

"Well, Mr Holmes?" said he.

But my friend's eyes were fixed upon the secretary, who stood by his master's chair.

"I think, your Grace, that I could speak more freely in Mr Wilder's absence."

The man turned a shade paler and cast a malignant glance at Holmes.

"If your Grace wishes—"

"Yes, yes, you had better go. Now, Mr Holmes, what have you to say?"

My friend waited until the door had closed behind the retreating secretary.

"The fact is, your Grace," said he, "that my colleague, Dr Watson, and myself had an assurance from Dr Huxtable that a reward had been offered in this case. I should like to have this confirmed from your own lips."

"Certainly, Mr Holmes."

"It amounted, if I am correctly informed, to five thousand pounds to anyone who will tell you where your son is?"

"Exactly."

"And another thousand to the man who will name the person or persons who keep him in custody?"

"Exactly."

"Under the latter heading is included, no doubt, not only those who may have taken him away, but also those who conspire to keep him in his present position?"

"Yes, yes," cried the Duke, impatiently. "If you do your work well, Mr Sherlock Holmes, you will have no reason to complain of niggardly treatment."

My friend rubbed his thin hands together with an appearance of avidity which was a surprise to me, who knew his frugal tastes.

"I fancy that I see your Grace's cheque-book upon the table," said he. "I should be glad if you would make me out a check for six thousand pounds. It would be as well, perhaps, for you to cross it. The Capital and Counties Bank, Oxford Street branch are my agents."

His Grace sat very stern and upright in his chair and looked stonily at my friend.

"Is this a joke, Mr Holmes? It is hardly a subject for pleasantry."

"Not at all, your Grace. I was never more earnest in my life."

"What do you mean, then?"

"I mean that I have earned the reward. I know where your son is, and I know some, at least, of those who are holding him."

The Duke's beard had turned more aggressively red than ever against his ghastly white face.

"Where is he?" he gasped.

"He is, or was last night, at the Fighting Cock Inn, about two miles from your park gate."

The Duke fell back in his chair.

"And whom do you accuse?"

Sherlock Holmes's answer was an astounding one. He stepped swiftly forward and touched the Duke upon the shoulder.

"I accuse *you*," said he. "And now, your Grace, I'll trouble you for that cheque."

Never shall I forget the Duke's appearance as he sprang up and clawed with his hand, like one who is sinking into an abyss. Then, with an extraordinary effort of aristocratic self-command, he sat down and sank his face in his hands. It was some minutes before he spoke.

"How much do you know?" he asked at last, without raising his head.

"I saw you together last night."

"Does anyone else beside your friend know?"

"I have spoken to no one."

The Duke took a pen in his quivering fingers and opened his cheque-book.

"I shall be as good as my word, Mr Holmes. I am about to write your check, however unwelcome the information which you have gained may be to me. When the offer was first made, I little thought the turn which events might take. But you and your friend are men of discretion, Mr Holmes?"

"I hardly understand your Grace."

"I must put it plainly, Mr Holmes. If only you two know of this incident, there is no reason why it should go any farther. I think twelve thousand pounds is the sum that I owe you, is it not?"

But Holmes smiled and shook his head.

"I fear, your Grace, that matters can hardly be arranged so easily. There is the death of this schoolmaster to be accounted for."

"But James knew nothing of that. You cannot hold him responsible for that. It was the work of this brutal ruffian whom he had the misfortune to employ."

"I must take the view, your Grace, that when a man embarks upon a crime, he is morally guilty of any other crime which may spring from it."

"Morally, Mr Holmes. No doubt you are right. But surely not in the eyes of the law. A man cannot be condemned for a murder at which he was not present, and which he loathes and abhors as much as you do. The instant that he heard of it he made a complete confession to me, so filled was he with horror and remorse. He lost not an hour in breaking entirely with the murderer. Oh, Mr Holmes, you must save him—you must save him! I tell you that you must save him!" The Duke had dropped the last attempt at self-command, and was pacing the room with a convulsed face and with his clenched hands raving in the air. At last he mastered himself and sat down once more at his desk. "I appreciate your conduct in coming here before you spoke to anyone else," said he. "At least, we may take counsel how far we can minimize this hideous scandal."

"Exactly," said Holmes. "I think, your Grace, that this can only be done by absolute frankness between us. I am disposed to help your Grace to the best of my ability; but, in order to do so, I must understand to the last detail how the matter stands. I realize that your words applied to Mr James Wilder, and that he is not the murderer."

"No; the murderer has escaped."

Sherlock Holmes smiled demurely.

"Your Grace can hardly have heard of any small reputation which I possess, or you would not imagine that it is so easy to escape me. Mr Reuben Hayes was arrested at Chesterfield on my information at eleven o'clock last night. I had a telegram from the head of the local police before I left the school this morning."

The Duke leaned back in his chair and stared with amazement at my friend.

"You seem to have powers that are hardly human," said he. "So Reuben Hayes is taken? I am right glad to hear it, if it will not react upon the fate of James."

"Your secretary?"

"No, sir; my son."

It was Holmes's turn to look astonished.

"I confess that this is entirely new to me, your Grace. I must beg you to be more explicit."

"I will conceal nothing from you. I agree with you that complete frankness, however painful it may be to me, is the best policy in this desperate situation to which James's folly and jealousy have reduced us. When I was a very young man, Mr Holmes, I loved with such a love as comes only once in a lifetime. I offered the lady marriage, but she refused it on the grounds that such a match might mar my career. Had she lived, I would certainly never have married anyone else. She died, and left this one child, whom for her sake I have cherished and cared for. I could not acknowledge the paternity to the world, but I gave him the best of educations, and since he came to manhood I have kept him near my person. He surmised my secret, and has presumed ever since upon the claim which he has upon me, and upon his power of provoking a scandal which would be abhorrent to me. His presence had something to do with the unhappy issue of my marriage. Above all, he hated my young legitimate heir from the first with a persistent hatred. You may well ask me why, under these circumstances, I still kept James under my roof. I answer that it was because I could see his mother's face in his, and that for her dear sake there was no end to my long-suffering. All her pretty ways, too—there was not one of them which he could not suggest and bring back to my memory. I *could* not send him away. But I feared so much lest he should do Arthur—that is, Lord Saltire—a mischief, that I dispatched him for safety to Dr Huxtable's school.

"James came into contact with this fellow Hayes because the man was a tenant of mine, and James acted as agent. The fellow was a rascal from the beginning; but, in some extraordinary way, James became intimate with him. He had always a taste for low company. When James determined to kidnap Lord Saltire, it was of this man's service that he availed himself. You remember that I wrote to Arthur upon that last day. Well, James opened the letter and inserted a note asking Arthur to meet him in a little wood called the Ragged Shaw, which is near to the school. He used the Duchess's name, and in that way got the boy to come. That evening James bicycled over—I am telling you what he has himself confessed to me—and he told Arthur, whom he met in the wood, that his mother longed to see him, that she was awaiting him on the moor, and that if he would come back into the wood at midnight he would find a man with a horse, who would take him to her. Poor Arthur fell into the trap. He came to the appointment and found this fellow Hayes with a led pony. Arthur mounted, and they set off together. It appears—though this James only heard yesterday—that they were pursued, that Hayes struck the pursuer with his stick, and that the man died of his injuries. Hayes brought Arthur to his public-house, the 'Fighting Cock,' where he was confined in an upper room, under the care of Mrs Hayes, who is a kindly woman, but entirely under the control of her brutal husband.

"Well, Mr Holmes, that was the state of affairs when I first saw you two days ago. I had no more idea of the truth than you. You will ask me what was James's motive in doing such a deed. I answer that there was a great deal which was unreasoning and fanatical in the hatred which he bore my heir. In his view he should himself have been heir of all my estates, and he deeply resented those social laws which made it impossible. At the same time, he had a definite motive also. He was eager that I should break the entail, and he was of opinion that it lay in my power to do so. He intended to make a bargain with me—to restore Arthur if I would break the entail, and so make it possible for the estate to be left to him by will. He knew well that I should never willingly invoke the aid of the police against him. I say that he would have proposed such a bargain to me; but he did not actually do so, for events moved too quickly for him, and he had not time to put his plans into practice.

"What brought all his wicked scheme to wreck was your discovery of this man Heidegger's dead body. James was seized with horror at the news. It came to us yesterday, as we sat together in this study. Dr Huxtable had sent a telegram. James was so overwhelmed with grief and agitation that my suspicions, which had never been entirely absent, rose instantly to a certainty, and I taxed him with the deed. He made a complete voluntary confession. Then he implored me to keep his secret for three days longer, so as to give his wretched accomplice a chance of saving his guilty life. I yielded—as I have always yielded—to his prayers, and instantly James hurried off to the 'Fighting Cock' to warn Hayes and give him the means of flight. I could not go there by daylight without provoking comment, but as soon as night fell I hurried off to see my dear Arthur. I found him safe and well, but horrified beyond expression by the dreadful deed he had witnessed. In deference to my promise, and much against my will, I consented to leave him there for three days, under the charge of Mrs Hayes, since it was evident that it was impossible to inform the police where he was without telling them also who was the murderer, and I could not see how that murderer could be punished without ruin to my unfortunate James. You asked for frankness, Mr Holmes, and I have taken you at your word, for I have now told you everything without an attempt at circumlocution or concealment. Do you in turn be as frank with me."

"I will," said Holmes. "In the first place, your Grace, I am bound to tell you that you have placed yourself in a most serious position in the eyes of the law. You have condoned a felony, and you have aided the escape of a murderer; for I cannot doubt that any money which was taken by James Wilder to aid his accomplice in his flight came from your Grace's purse."

The Duke bowed his assent.

"This is, indeed, a most serious matter. Even more culpable in my opinion, your Grace, is your attitude towards your younger son. You leave him in this den for three days."

"Under solemn promises—"

"What are promises to such people as these? You have no guarantee that he will not be spirited away again. To humour your guilty elder son, you have exposed your innocent younger son to imminent and unnecessary danger. It was a most unjustifiable action."

The proud lord of Holdernesse was not accustomed to be so rated in his own ducal hall. The blood flushed into his high forehead, but his conscience held him dumb.

"I will help you, but on one condition only. It is that you ring for the footman and let me give such orders as I like."

Without a word, the Duke pressed the electric bell. A servant entered.

"You will be glad to hear," said Holmes, "that your young master is found. It is the Duke's desire that the carriage shall go at once to the Fighting Cock Inn to bring Lord Saltire home.

"Now," said Holmes, when the rejoicing lackey had disappeared, "having secured the future, we can afford to be more lenient with the past. I am not in an official position, and there is no reason, so long as the ends of justice are served, why I should disclose all that I know. As to Hayes, I say nothing. The gallows awaits him, and I would do nothing to save him from it. What he will divulge I cannot tell, but I have no doubt that your Grace could make him understand that it is to his interest to be silent. From the police point of view he will have kidnapped the boy for the purpose of ransom. If they do not themselves find it out, I see no reason why I should prompt them to take a broader point of view. I would warn your Grace, however, that the continued presence of Mr James Wilder in your household can only lead to misfortune."

"I understand that, Mr Holmes, and it is already settled that he shall leave me forever, and go to seek his fortune in Australia."

"In that case, your Grace, since you have yourself stated that any unhappiness in your married life was caused by his presence, I would suggest that you make such amends as you can to the Duchess, and that you try to resume those relations which have been so unhappily interrupted."

"That also I have arranged, Mr Holmes. I wrote to the Duchess this morning."

"In that case," said Holmes, rising, "I think that my friend and I can congratulate ourselves upon several most happy results from our little visit to the North. There is one other small point upon which I desire some light. This fellow Hayes had shod his horses with shoes which counterfeited the tracks of cows. Was it from Mr Wilder that he learned so extraordinary a device?"

The Duke stood in thought for a moment, with a look of intense surprise on his face. Then he opened a door and showed us into a large room furnished as a museum. He led the way to a glass case in a corner, and pointed to the inscription.

"These shoes," it ran, "were dug up in the moat of Holdernesse Hall. They are for the use of horses, but they are shaped below with a cloven foot of iron, so as to throw pursuers off the track. They are supposed to have belonged to some of the marauding Barons of Holdernesse in the Middle Ages."

Holmes opened the case, and moistening his finger he passed it along the shoe. A thin film of recent mud was left upon his skin.

"Thank you," said he, as he replaced the glass. "It is the second most interesting object that I have seen in the North."

"And the first?"

Holmes folded up his cheque and placed it carefully in his notebook. "I am a poor man," said he, as he patted it affectionately, and thrust it into the depths of his inner pocket.